Keeping Mercy

In God's Keeping

Book 2

By

Ronna M. Bacon

ISBN 978-1-998821-46-4

Micah 6:8. He has shown you, O man, what *is* good; And what does the Lord require of you

But to do justly, To love mercy, And to walk humbly with your God?

Isaiah 30:18. Therefore the Lord will wait, that He may be gracious to you; and therefore He will be exalted, that He may have mercy on you. For the Lord is a God of justice; blessed are all those who wait for Him.

NKJV

Table of Contents

Stretching as he rose from his work bench in his taxidermist shop, Briar Koyle's hands reached towards the ceiling. He dropped his arms, his hands resting on the bench as he studied the fox pelt that he had been working on. The form was taking shape in a good way, he decided, before he turned as he heard a soft sound. He should be alone in the shop, he knew, and could not understand how there was any sound from the front reception area. Briar moved that way, searching for what made the sound. His keen gray eyes studied the area before he walked towards the door. He ran a hand through his brown curls, puzzled at what he had heard.

Spinning as he heard another soft sound, Briar searched the area before he moved towards where a form stood. He continued to frown as he came to a stop there, a hand reaching out to pull the person forward. Shocked, his hand dropped back to his side even as his other hand rested on his cheek. He stared at the lady and she was a lady who stood in front of him.

"Who are you? And why are you here?" Briar winced at the harshness of his voice. Having had his brother, Arlyn, go through danger had changed how he reacted in situations such as this.

The lady, dressed in a black pantsuit and white blouse with shoes that had a three-inch heel on them, shrank back from her. Her red hair curled around her face. Her deep brown eyes held her fear.

"I'm sorry. I shouldn't be here. I'll leave." She moved to pass him before his hand on her arm stopped her. "Please? Let me go."

"Not until you explain." Briar kept his hand on her arm, drawing her back into the work area. He shoved her into a chair before he stood in front of her, his eyes not moving from her face. "Explain why you're here." He frowned as he sensed that she was afraid. There should be nothing in his building that should cause that fear. "What are you afraid of?"

The lady shook with fear. She looked past him towards the door, fully expecting the men who had been chasing her to appear in the doorway. She had no idea what they wanted and hadn't waited around to find out.

"I'm sorry. I'll leave." She tried to rise, finding Briar's hand on her shoulder keeping her in her chair.

"I'm Briar Koyle. Can you tell me your name?" Briar's voice had softened as he spoke with a calm tone to it.

The lady stared up at him, uncertainty on her face. She suddenly decided to trust him. What could she lose?

"My name is Brynne Baker. I'm sorry. I was being chased and your door was open. I need to leave." Brynne was on her feet, moving past him, to once more be stopped by his hand on her arm. "Please? I need to leave. I am bringing danger to you, and I don't know why."

"I can help you with that. I don't want you to come to any harm." Briar began to pray for Brynne. "What do you think that you're in danger?"

"There were men chasing me just before I came in here. I've been followed for the last few weeks while I've been working and when I'm out and about. I need to stay safe. I just don't know how to do that." Brynne could not feel any anger about that. She was just too afraid.

"I can help you with that. I have a friend who is an investigator that we can talk with." Briar made a sudden decision. "I'm not letting you walk through this alone. Not now. Not ever."

Brynne stared at him, taking in his height and then the fierceness of his words. She frowned, not expecting that from a stranger.

"You can't do that." Brynne spun and ran for the outside door, Briar on her heels. She shoved open the door and flew through it, her heels clicking on the pavement before she froze. The men were waiting for her and that didn't seem to be good for her.

Briar had raced after her, coming to a sudden halt behind her. His hands reached to tuck her behind him, despite her protests.

"Hush, Brynne, if I can call you that." Briar's voice growled at her, stopping her words. "We need to determine what they want."

"They want me. I don't know why." Brynne buried her head against Briar's back, her hands clutching at his plaid flannel shirt. "Can we escape?"

—

Briar shook his head at her, his eyes not leaving the two men in front of him. He lifted his eyes to search for a way to escape, not seeing it. He began to back up, forcing Brynne to do so. He could hear her grumbling, a grim smile lighting his face for a moment. Briar did not take his eyes off the men, watching as they just stood in front of them.

Brynne felt the steps to the building hit her heel and began to climb them backwards, reaching for the door as she found the landing. Briar just moved with her, pulled by her grip on his shirt. He sighed to himself. He could lock them into the building but that would not solve the problem of them leaving. He slammed the door behind him, shooting home the locks and deadbolts. Moving to a window, Briar watched the men, seeing them walk towards his truck and then stand there.

Reaching for his phone, Briar made a call that he never expected to make. He called the emergency services for help. Unfortunately, it would take them a few moments to reach them, moments that he didn't know if they had.

"Briar? What do we do?" Brynne once more clutched at his shirt, not willing to move too far from him.

"I don't know." Briar watched as the men left, relief momentarily crossing his mind. "They've left."

"I see that but where are they? They won't leave me alone." Brynne paced the reception area, not taking in the stuffed critters and photos that lined the walls.

"Why are they after you? What do you do anyway?" Briar turned to face her, waiting for her to speak.

"I'm a wildlife technician." She frowned at him. "I know your brother."

"Which one? I have two. And yes, we're triplets." Briar grinned at her look.

"Cayce. He's the sculptor or carver, isn't he?"

"He is." Briar turned at he heard a sound before he leapt towards Brynne, taking her to the floor and covering her as best as he could with his body despite her frantic attempts to escape him.

The window near the door exploded inwardly as a gas canister flew through it. The escaping gas caused the couple to begin to cough wildly before they lay still, not moving even as the door was broken in, the locks hanging uselessly from the broken door jamb. The two men reached for the couple, one draping Briar over his shoulder, the other reaching for Brynne. They disappeared with them even as the lights and sirens of the responding police broke the silence around the building and lit up the late afternoon sky.

—

Chapter 2

The patrol officers spread out around the building and inside the building, searching for Briar. He was nowhere to be found despite how much he was searched for. Joe, a friend of the Koyle brothers and also a police investigator, had appeared, approaching the building. He frowned as he studied the door and then peeked inside. A hand went across his nose and mouth as he smelt the lingering odour of the gas.

"What do you know?" Joe turned to one of the first officers on the scene.

"Not a lot, Joe. Not a lot. Briar's not here. From the condition of the door, I would say that he's been taken somewhere." The officer frowned. "There was a lady in there. We found a lady's high-heel shoe in the reception area."

"He doesn't have any office help." Joe frowned at the words. "Who would she be?"

"Does he have security feeds?" The officer walked closer to the building to search. "He does."

"Yes, he does. After what Arlyn went through, all his family have increased their security presence." Joe was frustrated, to say the least. "I'll need to call one of his brothers or his father to see if they have access to the feed. They don't need this right now."

"No, they don't." The officer walked away, leaving Joe staring at the broken door and then pacing around the parking lot. There was just no sign of Briar and whoever the mysterious lady was. He reached for his phone, not sure which of the brothers to reach out to. He knew that their parents were out of town at a conference and weren't available. Arlyn won the coin toss and Joe dialed his number. "Arlyn? Where are you?"

"At home. I'm done work for the day. Why are you calling me?" Arlyn drew in a deep breath, his arm reaching for his bride, Skylor. "Which one?"

"Briar. He's disappeared from his work building." Joe held the phone away from his ear at Arlyn's explosive comment. "No, Arlyn. I don't have much information. What we need is access to his security feed."

"I can do that. We're on our way. I can pull it up on my phone." Arlyn pocketed his phone, reaching to hug Skylor.

"Arlyn? What happened?" Skylor shoved away from him, afraid for whichever one of her new family who was hurt.

"Briar. He's disappeared." Arlyn ran for his truck and tucked Skylor inside before he was heading for Briar's building. Forced to park down the street from it, he reached for Skylor's hand as they ran forward, seeing Joe waiting for them.

"Joe? Where is he?" Arlyn slid to a halt, feeling Skylor's hand tightening on his.

"I don't know, Arlyn. I really don't. We received a call for help from Briar. By the time the first officers arrived, he was gone." Joe frowned at Arlyn, not sure how to frame his next remarks.

———

13

"Who else was there, Joe?" Skylor's voice held conviction that someone else had become involved in the disappearance.

"A lady. We found one of her shoes in the reception area. A dress shoe. Briar wasn't dating, was he?" Joe didn't think that he was but as part of his investigation, he had to ask.

"No, he wasn't. He hadn't found anyone who he wanted to date." Arlyn was adamant about that. "Who is she?"

"I don't know. Her shoe didn't have a name in it." Joe's voice held a bite of anger. He was worried about his friend and the unknown lady.

"I see." Arlyn reached for his phone to scroll through his apps. He pulled up the security app for Briar's video feed and started to run it. "How far back do we need to go?"

"About an hour. Try that. If we need to, we'll go back further." Joe stood shoulder to shoulder with Arlyn, watching as the other man found the spot. They studied it together before Arlyn paused it.

"Who's that?" They watched as Briar pulled Brynne from where she had been hidden. "I don't recognize her."

Skylor reached to tilt Arlyn's hand as she frowned at the screen. She nodded.

"That's Brynne Baker. I know her from a Bible study at the church. She looks terrified."

"She does. Thank you for identifying her, Skylor. That helps." Joe walked away, his notepad

---

stuck back into a pocket, and with a request that Arlyn send him that section of the feed. He thought that he recognized the two men but would have the crime lab search them out. He had no doubt that they would put their best effort into it.

"Skylor? You really know her?" Arlyn stood and watched the activity, praying for his brother. He had prayed that his brothers would not face what he and Skylor had. It seemed as if God had other ideas.

"I do, Arlyn. Not as well as I would like to. You know how difficult it is for me to make friends." Skylor's past life of being held without contact with anyone else by an abusive father had led to her hesitancy in making friends.

"I know, sweetheart. I know. You're making strides that way. You just haven't found that one person to be a good friend for you." Arlyn turned as he heard footsteps. His other brother, Cayce, had approached him.

"Arlyn? What's going on? Briar didn't show for a meal. What's happening here?" Cayce stared at his brother and then at the scene around his brother's building.

"Briar's disappeared within the last hour. He's not alone. A Brynne Baker is with him." Arlyn turned as he heard a sound from Cayce. "Cayce?"

"Brynne Baker? Her father's one of the wealthiest ones in town. But I hear that she's estranged from him because she refused to let him dictate what she does."

"As in work?" Arlyn sighed as Cayce nodded. "What has Briar become involved in?"

"I have no idea, Arlyn." Cayce eyed Skylor. "Skylor?"

Skylor shook her head, watching the scene around Briar's building

"I don't know her well enough to know for sure that is the case. She has said some tidbits about her parents and I gathered that they weren't close." Skylor walked away, heading for Arlyn's truck. The men's aunt was waiting for her, wrapping her into a hug.

"Skylor? It's Briar this time?" Anna looked past her at her two nephews.

"It is, Aunt Anna. And I'm so afraid for him." Skylor's face was sober as she stepped back from the older lady. "This should not have happened."

Chapter 3

Anna watched her two nephews closely. The three men were close, probably closer than most given that they were triplets. She knew that their relationships were changing, given that Arlyn and Skylor were married. She also knew that the other two would not change that fact, wishing and praying instead for their own life mates.

"Cayce? What are your thoughts?" Ardan had stood beside his sister for a moment, an arm around her shoulders. They were both troubled by the fact that Briar was missing and perhaps even injured. They were praying for him, but also knew that they had to leave him in God's hands. God was in control and had Briar and Brynne in His hands, no matter where they were or what condition that they were in physically.

"My thoughts?" Cayce shook his head, dragging himself back from his thoughts. He was really worried about his brother, worried that he was hurt and that he would never come home. He didn't think that he could handle that. "I don't know what to think, Dad. I really don't. I don't know that we have enough information to even begin to start thinking anything other than that Briar is missing."

"There's that." Arlyn stood shoulder to shoulder with his brother. Skylor had disappeared with Bessie and he wasn't sure what she was up to, unless they were preparing a meal. Not that any of them felt like eating, he knew. "Dad? What do you know about the Bakers? I don't really know that much."

"The Bakers? Not a lot, just like you. They are prominent in town but no one knows much about them. They have just kept their lives quiet and hidden." Ardan was determined to find out what he could. "I don't know anything about their daughter."

"And I think that we will learn more about her given this situation." Cayce spoke up. He walked away. He found his mother waiting for him to give him a hug.

Bessie studied her youngest son. It was weighing heavily on him, she decided, whatever had happened to Briar.

"Son? You're worried but God is in control."

"I know, Mom. It's just so hard to trust at this time. After what Arlyn went through, I prayed that Briar and I would avoid anything. It didn't happen. Where is he?" Cayce was sober, his emotions raw on his face.

"I have no idea, Cayce. If I did, I would go and bring him home. No one knows at this point. And he will come home. I have that much confidence in that fact." Bessie walked away, worried more than she would admit.

Skylor walked to where she could watch the others, worried thoughts running through her mind. Just where was her brother-in-law? And just who was this lady who had disappeared from his building? She had watched Brynne, wanting to speak with her but her past life had driven the ability for the most part from her to speak freely with others.

Arlyn turned and then moved into her space, hugging her. He was worried about her, knowing that she would relive again and again the troubles that they had gone through.

"Skylor? What do you think?"

"What do I think?" At his nod, she sighed. "I have no idea other than Briar is missing as is Brynne. You know, I have wanted to speak with her. But I just couldn't. God knew that. I guess that at some point, we'll talk."

"We will. And you'll able to help her understand how God works in these situations. I hate that you have those words."

"I know that you do. God is here, isn't He? And He will protect them. I just want him here. You don't need this." Skylor was saddened at Briar's disappearance.

"No, none of us do. But it is what it is. We'll get through it and our friends will help just as they did when we went through our adventure." Arlyn didn't need to ask them. He knew that they would be there for them once more.

Joe approached the house, not sure what to say. There was no evidence of where the couple had been taken. The features of the men were not clear. They had made sure of that. All Joe knew for certain was that the couple were unconscious when they were removed and taken to a vehicle that had parked in such a way to obscure the license plate. It had been three days since Briar had disappeared, taking Brynne with him, or was it the other way around? Not one person was sure about that.

Ardan turned from the door, pointing towards the kitchen. It was where they always gathered with friends, a cup of coffee or tea and snacks shared with them. He was on his own at that point, Bessie out at a meeting and the boys at work. Anna had had to travel for a conference and would be away for a few days.

"Joe? What can you tell me?" Ardan sat, his head buried in his hands for a moment. He wanted his son home and would go and drag him back, if he only knew where he was. He had to release that desire to God and trust in God's mercies to bring him home once more.

"Not a lot, Ardan. I'm sorry. I have no idea where he is or if he's still with Brynne. There was just not enough evidence or information for us to find them." Joe was compassionate as he spoke. This family didn't need a second son facing danger and his worst thoughts were that Cayce would as well.

"Thank you for your honesty, Joe. That means a lot." Ardan frowned as he heard a sound at the door. There should be no one there. On his feet he headed that way, Joe at his heels with a hand on his police-issued weapon. Both men stopped short in shock as the door opened and Briar appeared, an arm around a lady. It had to be Brynne, they both decided.

"Briar? Son?" Ardan moved towards his son, catching him as he collapsed.

Joe moved in to catch Brynne before he headed for the living room to deposit her on a couch. He was

—

back to help Ardan raise Briar to his feet and to an upholstered chair in the room as well. Running outside, Joe searched for whoever it was that had brought Briar home. He found no one. His phone was out as he called for emergency services.

Ardan was standing staring between his son and the lady. He was overjoyed to see them but puzzled as well as how they had managed to make their way here. He would have thought that Briar would have headed for his own home.

Joe stood for a moment, staring at his friend before he walked over to stare down at Brynne. He could see the bruising on her face and frowned deeper. Someone had mistreated her, and he wanted whoever it was for treating a lady that way. His dark thoughts turned to prayer, begging God for answers and protection for these two.

Chapter 4

Ardan sat near his son, watching as he was assessed by a paramedic. He could faintly hear Briar's words and heard the protest that he was not going to the hospital, not unless Brynne was. And that was no guarantee. Brynne was awake and sitting up, frowning at the paramedic who was speaking with her. Ardan's attention went to her.

Brynne's brows were lowered as she angrily spoke to the woman. She was not going to the hospital nor was she going to her parents' home. That was simply not happening. And Brynne was too afraid to go to her own home. Her right hand curled over her left hand, hiding the ring that encircled her ring finger. She was ashamed about it and how it happened. Brynne glanced up to see Briar watching her, a shuttered look on her face. She saw the look in his eyes and frowned at him.

"Briar?" Joe's voice brought Briar's head around to face him. "Talk to me. Tell me exactly what happened? We had no idea what happened other than you two disappeared."

Briar shook his head. He was not ready to speak, and he knew that Brynne was not either. He would wait until they were alone with his father and Joe. And that should be soon. Both Briar and Brynne were wary of talking, not having had a chance to even discuss what had taken place that morning. He was on his feet and reaching for her hand, tugging Brynne to her feet and away from the others. The paramedics shared a

---

look and then left, taking the signed paperwork with them that the couple had signed to refuse transportation to the hospital.

Joe watched the couple flee and that was exactly what they were doing. He would grant them a few minutes and then bring them back to get their statements. Ardan was on his feet, watching his son walk away. He sighed to himself. There was something that Briar was hiding from him. This was what he had done as a teen, when he didn't want his father to know something. He would simply walk away, hoping that his father would never ask what the issue was.

Briar stopped Brynne by placing his hands on her arms. He didn't look at her, instead staring past her at the sky. He didn't know what to say or how to broach the subject with her that they were dancing around.

"Briar?" Brynne's voice was low and hesitant. "What do we do?" She had tears on her face and in her voice.

"Brynne? Are you okay?" Briar looked down at her and then hugged her, holding her as she wept.

"No, I'm not. This should not have happened." Brynne tried to move away from him but Briar would not let her. One of his hands reached to wipe at the tears. She looked up at him, seeing the compassion and caring on his face and something in his eyes that had her frowning at him.

"We need to speak with Joe." Briar was reluctant to move. When they did, it would change

—

everything. The happening from that morning was just too fresh and disturbing.

Brynne nodded. She knew that they needed to speak with the authorities. She didn't want to. She was too ashamed about the events. She felt Briar turning her back to the door and then felt his kiss on her temple. Brynne had no idea why he did that but it did bring comfort to her.

Joe stood in the kitchen, making fresh coffee, and turned his head to watch them. He frowned. He was positive that they were hiding something and what that something was he would definitely find out.

"Briar? Brynne? Into the living room. You need to talk to me and talk to me now." Joe's voice was stern. He would not allow them to run again. There were still officers outside of the house, kept there at Joe's request until he had a better sense of what had happened.

Briar nodded, his hand reaching for Brynne's. They walked into the living room, finding Ardan waiting for them. Ardan simply reached to hug his son, holding on to the man who stood so tall but feeling the uncertainty of a little boy in him. He then turned to Brynne, finding her watching him. He reached to hug her, not finding her responding. He hadn't expected that she would.

Sitting on the couch, Briar kept Brynne's hand in his. They needed that contact with one another, he knew, and felt her fingers tighten on his. They had no idea why the events had taken place or who the man behind it all was. Brynne was sure that it was her father. Briar just didn't know and told her as much.

Joe handed them their mugs of coffee, a frown on his face as he saw the ring on Brynne's finger. He knew that she was unmarried. That had been evident from his investigation. He didn't miss as she shifted closer to Briar, seeking comfort and protection from him.

"Briar? Talk to me. Tell me exactly what happened. We know that you were taken from your building." Joe reached for his notepad and pen, ready to make his notes.

"What happened to us?" Briar rubbed at his face with his free hand. His eyes were on Brynne, who had tipped her face so that she could watch him. There were some things that would not be told, at least not at the present time. "Where do I start?"

"Start with Brynne appearing in your building. I want to know why." Joe's voice was stern, almost harsh, causing Brynne to jump and then glare at him.

Briar drew in a deep breath, looking up to catch his father studying him and then studying Brynne. He knows, Briar decided.

"Okay, Joe. This is what happened up to when the gas came through the window." Briar documented the events, not taking his eyes away from looking at his father. "I don't remember when or how we were removed from the building. They used some sort of gas to knock us out."

Brynne was nodding as he spoke, confirming what he was saying.

"I ended up there, looking for somewhere to be safe. I had been running from someone and I don't even know who that someone was. Briar's building was the only one unlocked. I hid, hoping to find someone to help me. Briar found me and was trying to take me somewhere safe. It didn't work out that way." Brynne rubbed at her face, forgetting the ring on her finger. It glinted in the light, bringing eyes to her hand.

"Briar?" Ardan was on his feet, reaching for his son's hand. "What is this?" He knew that Briar had not been dating and here he was with a matching wedding band. "What did you do?"

Chapter 5

Briar drew in a deep breath. He had to continue their story and just didn't know how to do that. He knew also that he could not get away without confessing to how it had happened.

"Yes, Dad, we are married. I'll get to that." Briar bit at his lip, something that he only did when he was especially nervous and uncertain. He studied the lady sitting beside him, seeing an question in the eyes that he felt he was drowning in. "To go back to what happened to us. I don't know how they got us to where we woke up. We were in some big upholstered chairs. I was sprawled out in it. Brynne was crumpled in another chair. It was dark but I don't know how long it had been. I think sometime in the middle of the night. We weren't tied up or anything. Brynne was still out of it when I woke up. I just couldn't get up. I know that I wasn't awake for long before I slept again.

"I woke up again early in the morning. Brynne was awake and on her feet, searching for some way out of the room. I don't think that she found a way out. It was a study or office of some kind. Very opulent, I would say." Briar drew in a deep breath and took with thanks the bottle of water being handed to him. He prayed before he continued. He had no idea what the plan had been for them. "We both searched for a way out, even trying to open the windows and we couldn't do that. There was some food and water on the desk which we took, needing it."

Brynne's free hand reached for his and squeezed hard. She wanted to say something but waited for him to finish.

"A man finally unlocked the door and forced us out of there and into another room. It was small, with no furnishings. Just some blankets and pillows. It was on the first floor but again we couldn't get out of it. We were left there for that day and the next day. This morning? We were pulled out of there and forced back to the office. A man was there, waiting for us. He didn't say anything at first. We were forced to sit again in the chairs and forced to wait for what we weren't sure of."

Briar took a deep drink from the bottle of water and then rubbed at his cheek once more. He wasn't sure that what they had been asked to do was really factual or not.

"Finally, the man spoke. He wanted something from us. He informed us that we would be working for them. Brynne would find animals for them to trap and kill. I was to do the taxidermy work on the carcasses. The animals would then be used for smuggling. I refused as did Brynne. She took the brunt of his fury. I tried to get to her but three men held me back." Briar was beside himself that he could not help Brynne. He had been afraid that the man would kill her but the man had stopped after just a few moments. "It was at that point that we were forced to sign a marriage license application. We tried to refuse but the man held a gun to Brynne's temple. I don't think that we had any choice. Two men left with our identification and then came back with the license and a minister. Our identification was returned to us. We were forced through a marriage ceremony even as we protested. They just wouldn't listen to us."

Brynne was nodding, her vision clouded for a moment. Briar's words were just too true. They had been neglected and locked up for two days. They had spent time in conversation and also time in prayer. Briar had insisted on that. She knew that he regretted the ceremony but there hadn't been anything that they could do to prevent it.

"After a while, the men all left. We waited for a while, not willing to speak but afraid that they would come back. I finally tried the French door to the outside and it was unlocked. Brynne and I made our way out and then headed for here. I didn't want to go home and Brynne felt the same." Briar blinked at Joe, not sure if he had said everything that he needed to. He provided descriptions of the men, including the names that Brynne had whispered to him when they were left alone. He had not been prepared that information.

Joe looked over at Brynne, seeing the agitation that she was feeling.

"Brynne? Who were the men?" Joe waited almost impatiently for her to speak.

Brynne stared at him. She didn't know Joe, didn't know that he was a good friend of the brothers, and therefore, she didn't trust him. Her life had not been easy despite the wealth that she had been raised with. Walking away from it and from the parents who only paid attention to her when it would forward one of their plans had caused her to distrust people. She

—

looked up at Briar who gave her a small smile and a nod.

"The men? They work for my father. And these are their names." She provided the names. "And the house? It was one of my father's. He doesn't know that I found out that information years ago." She reached for a pad of paper and pen that sat beside the Bible on the end table and scribbled away. "Here. These are other places that he has and has hidden behind numbered companies. I have not seen my parents in ten years. I left as soon as I graduated high school and have not contacted them. I know that they are likely following me or having me followed. I don't want to see them or speak with them. Only God may have different plans for me."

Joe took the piece of paper. He had done a preliminary search of her parents and had not received the best vibes of who they were or what they did. He knew that it was old money that supplied some of their wealth but the rumours were that the father was involved in smuggling. What the couple had gone through confirmed that.

"So, what do we do with you two? You're not going to stay hidden. I know that much from what Arlyn and Skylor went through." Joe gave a grim smile. "And I know both of you will continue your work. Brynne? I would like to place an officer with you for the next while. I have officers volunteering to do that. The Koyle family supports our emergency forces and always have. They want to return the favour."

"I guess. I'm in the office some days but a lot of the time I'm out in the open and in the wilderness. I won't give that up. I can't. If I do, then they win. God help me, I don't want that. They've destroyed enough of my life." Brynne turned her face against Briar, feeling his hug.

Briar had an angry look on his face. He knew that God would protect them and had provided a way to do so. He just didn't want to do that. He knew that he would need to release his anger but didn't want to. Briar wanted to find the men responsible and make them pay for what they did.

Joe hesitated for a moment. The next questions would be touchy questions, ones that he never thought he would ever ask of one of his friends.

"Briar? Brynne? You're married. That changes what we do and how we protect you. What are your plans?"

Briar blinked and came back to the present. He had been plotting and planning revenge on Brynne's parents.

"What do we do? About being married?" At Joe's nod, he sighed. He had no idea what they would do. He only knew that he was not walking away from Brynne, not ever. And he looked up at that point to see his brothers, Skylor, his mother, and his aunt standing and staring at the couple in shock. They had not realized that the couple had returned to them.

Chapter 6

Briar's face tightened as he faced his family. His arm wrapped around Brynne and pulled her closer to his side. Brynne shrank back against him, staring at the people who had suddenly appeared. She frowned as she stared at Arlyn and Cayce and then up at Briar. She sighed. What kind of family had she just become part of? Brynne leaned harder against her groom, not sure if she should be speaking or not.

Bessie moved towards her son, finding him rising to hug her before his aunt moved in on him and then his brothers and Skylor. Bessie stared at Brynne before she was beside the younger lady and hugging her. She felt Brynne stiffen for a moment before Brynne hugged her back. She felt the sobs that shook Brynne's body and shot Briar a questioning look.

Briar moved away from the couch, letting his mother comfort his bride. Cayce and Arlyn drew him towards the hallway, watching as Skylor sank onto the couch beside Brynne, a hand on the other lady's back.

"Briar? When did you get home?" Arlyn kept glancing between Briar and Brynne.

"Not that long ago. Long enough to give Joe our statements." Briar blew out a breath. He felt God's hand on his shoulder, calming him. "Listen, guys. There's more than just us disappearing. Brynne and I were forced to marry this morning. It's a long story that I'll share but for now, I need to take care of her." Briar turned to move back towards Brynne, hesitating as he saw his female relatives surrounding her. "She's not had a good life. Her parents pretty much ignored her unless it was something that they wanted from her. She's been on her own since she was eighteen."

"She has? Well, she's not any longer. She's part of our family." Cayce was adamant about that. He prayed for his brother and his wife, knowing that their adventure was far from over. "What all can you tell us?"

Briar shrugged. He would share the story with them, and then they would all work on solving it. He also knew that their friends would become involved. In fact, he had sent an email to Levi Blackier or Blackie as he was called and his father, Samuel, who were private investigators. Blackie had sent back a quick email, just questioning if Briar was okay and then asking when they could talk.

"Brynne recognized the men who had kidnapped us. They work for her father. She thinks that her parents will deny that they sent them. Joe will contact them."

"They're out of town, Briar. I heard that on the street. They're on the run." Arlyn was angry as he realized that this was not over for his brother. "How do we do this?" He watched as Brynne struggled to her feet and then looked in panic for Briar, almost running into his arms. "What house was it?"

"One of theirs." Briar sighed. There was a lot that he didn't know and wanted to know but that would come with time. "Brynne? These are my brothers. Arlyn is married to Skylor, just as I told you. And

Cayce is the youngest of us. And yes, we are triplets. We talked about that.”

“We did.” Brynne turned in Briar’s arms, feeling safe with him and with his family. It was just that she was in a situation that she had never been in before. She had never been in a position where she felt loved so quickly and so safe. “Hi.”

“Welcome to the family, Brynne. We’ll work on finding your parents. I have been told that they are not in town.” Arlyn watched Brynne carefully, seeing the resignation on her face. “Brynne?”

“They have so many homes all over the place, not just here in Ontario but all over Canada but in other countries. I never questioned that. It was just life. I was never allowed to travel with them but I found documentation that I copied one day of their homes. They are under numbered companies.”

“And where is that documentation?” Joe had approached as he was leaving the home. “Can you tell me?”

“I can. It’s in a safety deposit box at a local bank. I didn’t want to leave it anywhere in my house. Someone has been in there recently. I was at a meeting for work that required me to dress up that day, Joe. That’s why I was in this.” She pointed at the suit that she was still wearing, as dirty and crumpled as it was. “I want to go home.” She spun Briar’s arms once more and clung to him, her eyes closing as she fought her emotions.

Joe grew angry once more. This should not be happening to this lady. She should be able to live her life without being followed and danger. She should have been able to make her own choice as to who and when she married. He sighed to himself. He was forgetting the sovereignty of God and how He had plans and purposes for their lives that they didn't know about.

"I'll take you there to retrieve the material." Joe frowned as Brynne shook her head. "Brynne?"

"I want to do that on my own, with just Briar. I need to take back my life. This is part of how I do that." Brynne stared at him, daring him to state otherwise.

Joe nodded, knowing that she needed to do that for her own sanity. He walked away, troubled by what had happened to his friend.

Briar turned Brynne to the back door and walked outside, his hand holding hers tight in his. He walked the back yard, letting her decompress as best that she could.

"Briar? Where do we go from here?" Brynne's voice trembled as she tried to think through the next steps.

"We decided where we live. First though, we need to stop by your home for you to grab some clothes. How good is your security system?" Briar had one of the best security systems that were available.

"Not that great apparently. Yes, I do need to improve it. It's a rental house." Brynne looked up at him. "You want me at your home."

—

Briar shrugged. They had to stay together and for now, it seemed that his home would be the best one.

"I do, Brynne. I really do. Just until we get this figured out. For now, we're married." Briar turned her back to where Cayce was waiting. "Cayce will give us a lift to your home and then to mine."

Cayce nodded, knowing that his brother wanted to head to his own home. He pointed to his truck and walked that way, hearing his brother's footsteps behind him. He was not surprised to see his father waiting for them.

Chapter 7

Briar walked through Brynne's home, liking the soft pastels that she had chosen for paint and the dark oak floors. He stood for a moment in her office, trying to determine exactly what she would need to take with her. Cayce stood beside him, not sure what to say. He could hear his father in the kitchen, looking through the kitchen and packing up the perishables and then working to tie up the garbage. That was what Ardan could do, leaving Briar and Cayce to deal with what they needed to.

Briar finally moved into the home office, reaching for Brynne's laptop and then searching for anything else that she would need. Brynne had explained what she needed for work and then for personal use. He felt uneasy doing that, feeling as if he was intruding on her privacy.

Brynne stood in her bedroom, a sob rising within her. She couldn't do this, she thought, but then stiffened her spine and reached for bags to pack her clothing. Brynne was sober as she did so, praying for God's peace within her. She knew that only He could give her the peace and confidence that she needed at that time. Reaching for her bags, Brynne carried them to the front door, frowning as she looked outside. Her car was in her driveway and she had no idea how that happened.

"Briar? My car's here. I had left it at the conference centre." Brynne leaned against Briar, drawing from his strength.

"It is? I'll let Joe know. Leave your keys and he'll have it towed to the police garage and go over it." Briar tucked away his phone, having reached Joe who promised to be there. He frowned at Joe's question as to where his truck was. It was not at his building. "Joe says that my truck is missing."

"It's at your home, Briar. We moved it there once we could access your building." Ardan stood behind his son. "Is something wrong?"

"There is. Brynne's car is here and it shouldn't be." Brynne was worried about that. "Are we ready to leave?"

"We are, son. Did you get everything from the office that Brynne will need?"

"I think so. Brynne, do you need to check?"

Brynne shrugged as she walked outside, bags in each of her hands. Her purse had appeared on her dresser and that frightened her, the thought that someone had been in her house more than just a little disturbing.

"I'll check later. For now, I just want a shower and to sleep." Brynne yawned widely. Briar watched her with compassion before he tucked her into Cayce's truck, helping to load everything into the box of Cayce's truck.

Walking through Briar's home, Brynne felt safe. She needed that at the moment. She turned her head as she could hear the three men discussing something and gave a small, sad smile. Brynne had never expected to marry and certainly not marry in such a way. Brynne headed for the home office, searching through what Briar had packed for her. She smiled wider. Briar had everything that she had needed and more than she had asked him to. She was grateful for that. Brynne pulled out her laptop and booted it up, signing into the wireless internet with the password that Briar had provided for her. She was soon deep into emails, forgetting that she had wanted a shower and a meal and then to sleep.

Briar came looking for her about an hour after she had sat down. He stood in the doorway, searching the room, trying to determine if she would be content to work there. Briar approached her, sitting beside her on the couch and just waiting for her to speak.

"Brynne?" Briar's voice broke through the concentration that Briar had become involved in.

Brynne looked up, startled and surprised to see him sitting beside her. She sighed. She had a tendency to get lost in her work when she was answering emails. There were two that frightened her with their threats, and Brynne had no idea what to do with them.

"Briar? Where did you come from?" She frowned at him. "You've cleaned up."

"I have. You should as well but what is troubling you? I can tell that something is." He took the laptop that she was thrusting at him. "What is wrong, love?"

"There are two emails that are threatening me. They've been sent to my work email. What do I do with them?" Brynne shook slightly with the strength of the fear that hit her.

"We'll pass them on to Joe. He'll have the crime lab take a look at them." Briar was quiet as he read the emails before he sent them on to Joe. He then saved Joe's contact information into her email program. "If you receive anything more like this, send it on to Joe." He reached for her phone as well, programming in Joe's information to her contacts. "Here, his information is on your phone as well." Briar hesitated before he continued to program in numbers. "I've put all of our numbers in for you."

"Thank you." Brynne was on her feet, heading for the bedroom that she had chosen. She looked around at the sage walls and cream trim and loved the colours. Reaching for clean clothes, Brynne headed for the ensuite, finding it roomier and more luxurious appearing that her own bathroom was and certainly better than the bathroom that she had had to use during her time at her parents' home.

Briar watched her walk away, on his feet to follow her to the hallway. He nodded even as he pulled out his phone. Joe had received the emails. Just what had Briar become involved in? Briar shrugged. He had no idea what he had become involved in. He wanted it over so that he could go on with the lady God had sent into his life. He knew in his heart that he would never walk away from Brynne. Not ever. Not even if she walked away from him.

Returning to the kitchen, Briar reached for the soup that he had heated and dished it out, setting the bowls on the table. He was uncertain if this would do for Brynne, having no ideas of her likes and dislikes.

—

All he knew was that he wanted to ensure that she was taken care of.

Brynne rubbed at her wet hair and then searched for her blow dryer. She had forgotten it and that frustrated her. She walked from the bedroom, searching for Briar, coming to a halt to stand and watch him as he worked in the kitchen. This was a sight that was unusual for her. Her father had never worked in the kitchen. Instead, he insisted that he be served.

Turning as he heard footsteps, Briar reached for Brynne, giving her a hug before he sat her at the table, pulling her chair back for her. He then sat beside her, reaching for her hand as his head bent to asking a blessing on their food. He bit at his lip before he begged God to protect them and solve this mystery quickly.

Chapter 8

The next day was a Saturday. Brynne was on her feet early, walking through the house, not finding Briar up yet. She sighed as she stared at the clock. It was too early, she decided, reaching to make herself a cup of tea and then finding a seat in the living room. Her Bible was in her hand, a pen beside her as she searched for all passages that spoke of mercy. Brynne had no idea why she was searching for that particular word, but God was leading her to do that. She knew that at some point He would reveal the reason why.

Briar stood for a moment before he joined her on the couch. He didn't say anything, not wanting to disturb her study. He saw the moment that Brynne realized that she was not on her own and saw the frightened look that briefly fluttered across her face. Briar wanted to take that from her but had no idea just how he could do that.

"I'm sorry. I disturbed you." Briar was contrite at that.

"It's okay. I'm just reading through on God's mercy. It is fascinating, you know." Brynne stared at her Bible. "What are we up to?"

"I'm not sure. I have to do some grocery shopping. Dad looked out for the perishables in your fridge. But you have food in the freezers."

—

Brynne sighed. She did indeed have food that she needed to clear out, that is, if she were to be living here.

"You're sure about this, Brynne? We don't know each other very well. I know that we talked during those couple of days and shared a lot. We still have a lot to share. I suggest that we set up a time for Bible study and prayer together. That will help us get through what we are facing. And it is far from over. I know that from what Arlyn and Skylor went through."

"How did they ever do it? And how did you all cope?" Brynne shifted so that she was facing him, eager to hear what he had to say.

"God, I guess." Briar thought back through the weeks of danger and uncertainty that their family had faced. "God provided for us. We didn't necessarily like what was happening but it was in His plan. I know someone who always says that God had plans and purposes for us that we don't understand yet. We may never know why on earth, but He is there every step of the way. Even when the darkness seems to be so heavy and we don't think that He hears our cries, He is right there beside us. It will grieve Him that we face danger but He has conquered it all. He knows how we will react." Briar's finger tapped at her Bible. "This is our guide book. We need to trust Him, no matter how hard it is."

Brynne was nodding. She had not been raised by her parents to think that but an old friend, a lady who had since passed to glory, had found her one day, led her to putting her trust in God, and mentored her for years. Brynne had moved in with her once she had escaped her home.

"It is so hard, Briar. I don't like that we had to marry in this way." She stared at her ring. "This is not the type of ring that you would have chosen. At least, I don't think so."

"You are correct. I suggest that we find rings that are more suited for us. I think that Joe will need these rings." Briar stared at his ring, suddenly afraid that he was being tracked by it.

"You think a tracking monitor of some kind?" Brynne had read his thoughts correctly.

"I do, Brynne, and that frightens me. You're out there on your own when working. You told me that." Briar began to fret about that.

Brynne's hand landed on his arm, bringing his gaze back to her.

"Joe sent me a text message. He has officers who will go with me when I'm out in the field. And he will have someone with me when I'm in the office. The same goes for you." Brynne frowned. "I really don't know much about what you do."

"No, you don't. Let's head out for breakfast and then find a jewelry store. I should stop by the building. I left a fox pelt that I had been working on and I need to see what happened to it." Briar was on his feet, drawing Brynne up with him and then towards the door. Brynne had barely time to catch at her purse before he had them out of the front door, the security system set, and the door locked behind them.

———

Briar stood two hours later at the counter of a jewelry store. His high school friend stood across from him, waiting patiently for Briar to decide on what ring he wanted. Jim had frowned when Briar asked for the wedding bands, not knowing the story of what had transpired for his old friend.

"I'm married, Jim, not by choice. We're going through an adventure similar to what Arlyn and Skylor did." Briar had watched as Jim had frowned and then nodded. "This is Brynne, my bride."

Jim had looked at Brynne, recognizing her from church. He didn't know her very well, in fact, knowing that not one of the group that they belonged to did. He had a feeling that was about to change and change quickly.

"Brynne? You're okay?" Jim's soft question had startled Brynne before she shrugged and nodded. "Okay, then, Briar. What are your thoughts?"

Briar had given him a quick glance before he searched the rings, finding a matching pair in rose gold that he pointed to. They were engraved and that suited him just fine. Brynne had begun to shake her head and stopped as Briar nodded. They were just what he wanted for her.

Turning to the engagement rings, Briar had studied those, hearing Brynne's low protest. He had shaken his head at her before choosing a beautiful blue diamond in a rose gold band. This was her, he decided.

Walking away from the store with the rings tucked into a pocket, Briar had helped Brynne into his truck. They were being watched and followed, he knew, and decided that for the present, he really didn't care. He was with a beautiful lady who just happened to be his wife. God was in control, and nothing would happen to them that day without God allowing it. Briar pulled away from the streets downtown and headed for his building. He needed to be there, just to assure himself that all was well.

Chapter 9

Briar unlocked his building door, hesitating before he pulled it open. The events that had happened there earlier in the week were still raw in his memory. He waited for Brynne to enter, seeing her hesitancy as well. Stepping into the reception area, Briar looked around. He gave a deep sigh of relief. His family had been around and tidied it up.

Walking through to his work shop, Briar stared around there. The fox pelt had been dealt with as if he had done that. He knew it was one of his brothers who had taken care of it. That relieved his mind. Briar turned as he felt a hand on his arm, reaching to hug Brynne. She was unsettled, he could tell, being back where it had all started.

"Okay, love?" Briar waited patiently for Brynne to respond.

"I think so. Are you?" Brynne felt his nod against the top of her head. "Can you work here still?"

"I think so. God is here as well, Brynne, and is with us wherever we go." Briar studied her face, seeing a peace there that had not been present earlier. "Let's change our rings and leave the old ones here. Joe will come by and pick them up next week." He pulled out the rings, waiting as she removed the plain gold band even as he did the same. He kissed her finger before he slid on the rings and then held out his for her to do the same to his finger. They both could feel the presence of God in the room with them.

Walking away from the building, Briar stood for a moment, his face tilted up. They had the rest of that day and Sunday to get through before they would both be back at work. He had no idea what Brynne's schedule was for the week.

"We need to talk, Brynne, about our schedules."

"We will, Briar. For now? Can we just go to your home? I want to do some research."

"Our home, Brynne. It's our home. And yes, we can do that." Briar watched the truck following him, not sure if it was friend or foe. He pulled into his driveway. The truck flashed its lights at him as it continued by. He drew in a deep breath. Joe had made arrangements for that. Briar would need to find him and thank him.

Brynne paced the house. She didn't know it and the creaks that sounded frightened her to some extent. She thought that they were normal for the house but until she had lived there for a while, she could not say for sure that they were normal. Briar was on a phone call, she could tell, hearing his voice from the office. Brynne did not want to intrude and therefore avoided that area of the house. The fridge door was opened as she glanced at the clock, knowing that they would need to eat soon. She just wasn't hungry. Besides that, Brynne did not know what Briar liked to eat although the food choices from earlier that day showed that their tastes in food were similar.

Briar approached Brynne, reaching to wrap her into a hug. He felt her jump and then relax. He would

<hr>

need to take it slow with her, he decided, not wanting to scare her totally away from him.

"Anything interesting in the fridge?" Laughter underlined his words.

Without thinking, Brynne elbowed him in the stomach. A hand to her mouth, she spun in his arms, horrified at what she had done. Brynne was not expecting Briar to simply hug her tighter and tell her it was perfectly fine to tell him off that way. He was well aware that was not how she was raised but it was how he was raised, so he took no offence at that action.

"Thank you, Briar. I just didn't think when I did that. I didn't have the relationship with anyone like you have. I don't know how to act." Brynne was matter-of-fact as she said that.

"Talk to Skylor. She's a good source for you to talk with. She was kept isolated her whole life with only contact with an abusive father. She's grown a lot since she and Arlyn met, but she still has days when she regresses." Briar was saddened by those days but knew that it would be something Arlyn and Skylor would need to deal with for years.

"She didn't? I will speak with her. At least I had contact with the servants and those at school." Brynne frowned at him. "I remember you and your brothers from school. I just never thought that I would ever speak with you let alone be married to you." She continued to frown as his face sobered.

"I remember you too, Brynne. I always wanted to be your friend but you never stayed around for very long. I guess I was too shy to come up and speak with you."

"I wish you had. Maybe we wouldn't be facing what we are." Brynne was thoughtful.

"I think that we still would have. God didn't mean for us to meet until now. There is a purpose for what we're going through." Briar reached past her for a package of chicken, intending on heading for the grill on the back deck. "How does chicken and a salad sound?"

"Sound about right." Brynne moved away from him, plucking out the lettuce and other vegetables that she needed for the salad. She worked about soberly, her thoughts troubled. Brynne wanted this over so that they could move on. Only that didn't seem about to happen.

Briar walked through the house late that night, ensuring that everything was locked up tight for the night. He paused at the closed bedroom door which Brynne had chosen, a hand resting on the door as he prayed for her.

Brynne raised her head from the pillow as she heard Briar pause at her door and then laid her head back down as she slept. She felt protected and safe.

Briar did not sleep that night. His mind was too active for that. He replayed their captivity over and over, puzzled at that last morning when they were just able to walk out of the house. That should not have been possible. He finally slept as morning crept into the sky, not hearing Brynne as she rose and tapped at his door as the morning grew late.

Brynne was distraught. She could not rouse Briar and refused to enter his bedroom. She turned as she heard a tap at the front door and crept that way. Peeking out of the window, she saw Arlyn and Skylor standing there, bags of what she assumed to be food in their hands. Brynne quickly deactivated the security system and opened the door, surprised to find herself hugged. She was not used to that.

"Where's Briar?" Arlyn looked around for him.

"I think that he's still sleeping. His door is closed." Brynne stared back towards the bedrooms. Briar had a sprawling bungalow with four bedrooms. They were located at one end of the house with the kitchen in the middle of the home.

Arlyn nodded and walked towards his brother's bedroom, tapping lightly at the door before he opened it and peeked in. Briar had not stirred, Arlyn could tell, before he walked into the room and gently shook his brother.

Briar jumped before he sat up abruptly, his eyes searching for whoever it was that had threatened him. He glared at Arlyn for a moment before he caught sight of the clock. He sighed. Brynne was likely up and he should be too.

"You awake, Briar?" Arlyn watched his brother closely, seeing the changes that were happening in him.

"I am now. Is Brynne?"

Arlyn nodded before he walked towards the door.

"She is and is anxious. You need to get up, Briar, and relieve your lady's mind. You need to do this." Arlyn walked out of the room, leaving Briar to sit on the side of the bed and stare at the closing door.

Chapter 10

Late that afternoon, Briar walked around his property, eyeing the trees that lined the edges of it and grew along the back. There were many. He usually enjoyed the privacy and enjoyment that they brought. Today, he was not so comfortable with them. Although there was an area cleared around the house, Briar was well aware that the men targeting them could very well approach the house easily. That made him afraid and not much did that to him. Briar turned to find Brynne beside him, worry on her face.

"Briar? How safe are we?" Brynne kept looking around, sensing someone in the woods watching them.

"As safe as we can be, I guess. I have someone I know who can come out and go over our security with us. He'll do that next week." Briar studied Brynne, seeing the shadows in her eyes. "What can I do for you, Brynne?"

Brynne shrugged. She had never had anyone other than the older lady who took her in ask her that. She didn't know what to say.

"I don't know, Briar. I really don't know. I don't know that anyone has ever really asked me that or cared what really happened to me." Brynne's voice held no censure of those who had not intervened or sought to help her. "God has been there for me and that has been sufficient. Until now."

"Until now?" Briar was shocked. It was not how he had been raised or how he reacted to anyone. "From now on, you are important to us. We will ask and keep asking what we can do for you. If you don't tell us, we will just step in. It is how we are God's hands and feet on earth." He spun in a circle, hearing faint rustling and knowing that it was not an animal. Briar reached to grab for Brynne's hand, running towards the house before he slammed the door and locked it behind them. He then stood with a hand on the door, watching out of the window.

Brynne stared at him in shock, her mouth opening and closing. She had no idea what had just taken place but obviously something or someone had been out there.

"Briar? Was that really necessary?" Brynne's voice was angry just because she was scared.

"It was. Someone was out there, Brynne. I couldn't see them but I could hear them. We would have disappeared again, I think, if we had not come back." He sighed as he turned to face her, his back against the door. "How do we keep you safe, Brynne? I don't want you to disappear on me. My heart couldn't take it." Briar wasn't aware that he was baring his heart to her, laying out his hopes and dreams for them as a couple.

"There was? I didn't know that." Brynne blinked rapidly, not sure what to think.

"There was. We need to make some plans, Brynne. I just don't know how to do that." Briar sighed as he felt his phone chiming. He refused to pull it out, despite the frown Brynne was sending him.

"Your phone? Briar, are you not going to answer it?" Brynne finally reached for where it was in a holster on his belt and thrust it at him. Briar almost dropped it.

"I won't when I'm with you, not unless I am expecting a call. You are that important to me." Briar stared at her until she nodded before he glanced at the phone and read the text message. A friend was reaching out to him, asking if he was okay and would he be home tomorrow night? He sent a quick text indicating that they would be, leaving his friend to send back a text message containing just question marks.

Brynne was frustrated and walked away from Briar. She didn't know how to respond to him. She had had little contact with men, other than those that she worked with, and she didn't have contact with them outside of work.

Briar sighed as he watched her walk away. This was all so new to him, and he felt like a fish out of water. He had no idea what to do or say. Everything he said or did seemed to be wrong. Briar reached for his phone as it rang, frowning at it. He ignored the call from his friend, heading instead to find his bride.

Brynne had found a seat on the side of her bed, her hands folded in her lap. Her eyes were on the floor as she soberly thought through her life as it was now. She had not envisioned her life to be like this. Brynne felt the bed sink beside her and a shoulder touch her. She glanced to her right. Briar had found her and

---

silently sat beside her, his arm tight to her shoulder. Brynne expected him to speak but he didn't.

"Briar? What do we do?" Brynne finally broke the silence between them.

Briar shrugged before he just began to pray for her and then for them as a couple. He brought in all the verses that he could think of that mentioned mercy and God's mercy.

Brynne began to relax, finding peace in the midst of their danger. She leaned harder against Briar, finding his arm coming around her. She was falling in love, she decided, with this tall handsome knight. He was the one who she had pictured all of her life.

Briar's voice finally ceased his prayer, his head not raising. He waited but what he was waiting for, he wasn't sure. God was working in their lives and was protecting them but he knew also that God's plans and purposes would be evident when His timing was right.

Brynne rose at last, walking away once more from Briar and heading for the office. She reached for some of the paperwork that they had been researching that day with his family. She thought back over the day, a small smile lurking on her face. While there had been concentrated research, there had been many times of lightness and laughter. She had felt as if she belonged, finally, in a family.

Briar stood at last, moving towards the kitchen, an eye on the clock. He knew that they had to eat but neither of them had much appetite. This was not how he had ever expected to start married life, if he had even thought that far. Setting their plates of salads on

---

a tray, he sliced fresh bread and set that plate and the butter dish on the tray as well. He reached for bottles of water and then headed to find Brynne.

"Brynne? Let's eat and set aside what we were working on. We need to do that. We'll solve it." Briar reached for the paperwork and set it aside despite her grumbling at him. He handed her the plate of salad and reached for his own.

"I have a friend coming tomorrow, Brynne. He'll bring his wife. Blackie, as we call him, is a private investigator. He and his wife, Julia, had an adventure as we call it, as did some of their friends. He'll look through what we've found and then begin his own investigation." His finger on her lips silenced her protest. "He won't share us for this. They do it for free for their friends."

Brynne was silent, not sure what to say. She had not expected this but knew that God would and could work in these ways. She sighed to herself. Life had suddenly gotten so hard and out of control. How was she to live her life with this going on? Brynne said as much to Briar.

Briar grinned at her before he reached for his own bottle of water to take a sip from it. He had expected that reaction from her. He hugged her before he reached to pick up the tray and carried it to the kitchen, returning with two bowls of ice cream.

Brynne stared at him and then at the ice cream. She shrugged at that and took the bowl offered to her. Whatever, she decided. She was soon lost in thought, not seeing the looks that Briar kept sending her way.

—

She set the bowl to one side before reaching for the top paper on the pile.

"Briar? Who is this?" Brynne thrust the paper at him.

"Who's who?" Briar took it, frowning at it. "This man? He runs the local humane society. Didn't you know that?"

Brynne shook her head. She didn't know that. She had no reason to know anything about the humane society. Her hand froze as an awful thought came to her.

"Briar? How many wild animals would they take in?" She was almost afraid to look at him.

Briar shrugged. It wasn't something that he had ever really thought about. Then he caught the drift of her question and paled.

"I don't know but we'll find out. Are you thinking what I think you're thinking?"

"That they are using the animals and wild animals at the shelter for nefarious reasons? Yes." Brynne sighed. This was not what she wanted to think but it had to be looked into, she knew.

Chapter 11

The next afternoon, Brynne trudged through the garage and into the house, shutting the door behind her. Her brown hiking boots hit the tray in the mudroom even as her jacket was hung on a hook. Brynne reached for a bottle of water from the fridge on the way by before she headed for the office, her backpack dropped onto the couch. She felt tired, dusty, and upset. Brynne had felt followed all day, despite the fact that an officer had been with her. What that man's presence had meant to the day? She was never sure, certain that if he had not been there, she would have disappeared and not been seen again.

Showered and dressed in clean and casual clothes, Brynne squinted at the clock. She had no idea when Briar would be home. They hadn't even discussed that and that frustrated Brynne. There was just so much that she didn't know about her groom and she didn't think that she had that much time to learn it.

Reaching for her backpack, Brynne pulled out the mail she had found in the mail box at her home. Carrying it in her hand, she walked through the house to the front door and reached into the box for Briar's mail. She then headed for the kitchen, dropping the mail on the table as she searched the fridge and freezer for something for a meal for them. Brynne knew that his friends were heading there. She just didn't know if they were expected for a meal and what they would eat. It was not usual for Brynne to be this upset over a meal but she was. It seemed everything was coming down on her and she felt as if she was drowning under it all.

Turning as she heard the door open to the mudroom, Brynne frowned for a moment before she moved to where she could see Briar. He looked exhausted, she decided, and knew that it wasn't just from his work.

"Briar?" Brynne's voice was hesitant as she saw his head come up and then a smile cross his face.

Briar was into the kitchen, hugging his bride, a kiss dropping on her temple. He had convinced himself that she had disappeared over the day and that he would be coming home to an empty, lonely house.

"You're here!" Briar leaned back to look down at her, a smile creasing his face.

"I am. And so are you. Did you expect that I wouldn't be?" Brynne was disgruntled at his words and it showed.

"I was praying that you had been safe all day. It's just everything I guess that's weighing down on me." Briar hugged her again before he leaned back once more. "Blackie and Julia are in town. They're picking up something for us to eat. It's what they do." He could see the relief that crossed her face. He looked past her to the table where the mail still lay. "You've retrieved the mail?"

"I did, both mine and yours. I haven't even looked through it yet. There could be threats contained in it and I wouldn't know that."

"We'll look through it." Briar finally walked away to change into casual clothes, returning to find Brynne staring down at the mail. She had apparently sorted it but had made no move to open it. "Brynne? What did you find?" He looked over her shoulder, seeing the plain white envelopes that she had set to one side.

"Those. I have looked at them. I have four in my box. There were two in yours. Who is doing this?" She leaned against him for a moment. "And your friends will be here soon."

"Yes, they will. Let's set these aside until Blackie gets here. He'll look them over. Then, we'll pass them on to Joe. He'll have his team look through them and see what they can determine about them."

Levi Blackier, or Blackie as he was called, watched his friend closely. He could see the fine lines of stress and strain that were developing on his face. His attention turned then to Brynne who was talking with his wife, Julia. He frowned. He knew her name but just not why.

"Briar? What can you tell me?" Blackie kept his voice low, not wanting to disturb the ladies who by that time was setting out the meal that Blackie and Julia had brought with them.

"Blackie? What can I tell you? I have no idea where to start. I'm afraid that I'm off on an adventure such as Arlyn had. I can tell you what happened to us. Brynne found a number of unmarked envelopes in our mail boxes today. We have not looked at them as of yet."

Blackie nodded. He had wondered if that was the case. He reached to lay a hand on Briar's shoulder as he prayed for the couple.

"Let's eat then, Briar, before we spend some time in prayer. Then, I want to hear whatever you can tell me." Blackie grinned at Brynne as she frowned at him.

"Okay, we eat then." Brynne sat beside Briar, not sure how to act or what to say. She remained fairly quiet as the other three spoke with one another.

Julia was watching Brynne closely as well, seeing the stress that the other lady was under. She sighed. She needed to find the words to draw Brynne out. She just didn't know if she could do that.

Brynne finally sat back down, the letters in front of her on the table. She had listened as Briar and she were prayed for as Blackie petitioned God on their behalf. She was growing in her walk with God as she spent her time with Briar. He was not afraid to tell her what he thought and what he thought God was doing in their lives.

"Okay, Briar. What do we have with those letters?" Blackie had pulled on latex gloves and reached for them, opening them one at a time. He frowned at them before he looked at the couple waiting expectantly for him to speak. "They're blank, guys. That is bizarre."

"Blank?" Briar was startled but also puzzled. "Who does that?"

Blackie shrugged before his phone was out and he was calling his father. Samuel had seen something like this in the past, and Blackie wanted to hear his father's thoughts on this. Samuel was not surprised to hear of the letters but asked Blackie to examine them carefully before turning them over to Joe. There just might be something there.

Briar was puzzled by the letters. He had expected threats but not blank pages. He shared a look with Brynne who simply shrugged. Brynne was not expecting the blank pages either but she knew that God had allowed them to appear. They just needed to figure out what they meant at some point.

Chapter 12

Late that night, Brynne snuggled down under her blankets. She had not really found that they had really gotten that far ahead in their research. She just wished it was over, she decided.

Briar had found his desk chair, his head bowing over his Bible. He needed that comfort from God's Word but he was also worried about Brynne. He too had prayed for more information to be forthcoming, but it wasn't. Briar finally raised his head, a sense of peace from God wafting through his heart. He reached for the paperwork that he had dropped there, reading back through it. Joe had been around and taken the envelopes and their contents. He too was puzzled at the papers.

Blackie had promised to be back in touch, sharing a look with Julia as he did so. He had set up a meeting with his father and also with his friend, Simon, a retired police officer who now worked for Samuel. He knew that they would work together to determine just who and what would be the answers for Briar and Brynne.

Two days later, Brynne raised her head, her attention on the hallway outside of her office. She was in the building that day. She frowned and then reached for her backpack and crept to the window. She opened it, shoved out the screen, and then dropped to the grass. She quickly shoved the screen back into place before heading for the corner of the building. Brynne carefully peeked around the corner and studied the parking lot. Seeing no one there, she ran for her car and quickly drove off. She just had no idea where to head.

Bessie approached their front door, frowning. She was not expecting anyone to appear. Opening it, Bessie stared at Brynne before she was reaching for the younger woman and drawing her into a hug. The front door was shut and locked behind Brynne.

"Brynne? What is wrong? You're shaking!" Bessie didn't release her. Instead, she directed her to the kitchen and gently shoved her into a chair.

"Someone was outside my office. I felt so afraid." Brynne wrapped her arms around herself, fear causing her to shake.

"What? How did you get away?" Bessie reached for bottles of juice and handed one to her daughter-in-law.

"I went out of the window." Brynne didn't see anything odd about that. It had been her one way of egress and she had taken it. "I need to call Joe."

"You do." Bessie reached for her phone on the table and sent a message to Joe. She shot a quick look at Brynne before she sent a text off to Briar, simply telling him that Brynne was with her and had been badly frightened.

Briar stared at his phone and then around his work shop. He had just tidied away what he was working on and had been planning on working in his office. Briar was on his feet, locking up his building

—

65

and then running towards his truck to head for his mother's and to find his wife.

Brynne jumped as she felt an arm around her. Her head spun around and she ended up nose to nose with her groom. She frowned at him, wondering how he knew where she was. She then looked past him to see Joe heading for the coffee pot, a grin on his face as she frowned at him. Brynne sighed and then thanked Bessie. She had been so frightened that she hadn't been aware that Bessie had reached out to the two men.

"Okay, love?" Briar studied her and saw that she was still frightened.

Brynne shrugged. She was still frightened but felt safer now that Briar was with her. She glanced back at Joe, finding him waiting for her to speak.

"Joe? What do I do? There was someone outside of my office door not that long ago. There should have been no one there other than a few workers. I didn't recognize the voice." Brynne rubbed at her face. She had no idea who that man had been.

Joe nodded. He had reached out to her supervisor and had spoken with that man. He had been surprised that Brynne had taken the way out of the building that she had but he knew who the man had been. It had been someone who worked for her father and had wanted access to her office. That had been refused and the man had been removed from the building and told not to come back.

"I know who it was, Brynne. He works for your father. Have you ever seen this man?" He slid a picture across the table. The man had a criminal record, which had not surprised Joe.

Brynne refused to look at the photo. She instead kept her eyes on Joe, not wanting to know for sure that the man was an employee of her father. Brynne finally sighed and looked down. She shook her head. She had no idea who that man was.

"I'm sorry. I don't recognize him. Should I?" Brynne felt Briar's arm around her and leaned against him.

"You should. He'll be back around and looking for you. He should not have been in that building, Brynne, and he was. Your supervisor stopped him, recognizing that he was out of place. This places all of you in danger."

"I know." Brynne was sober as she looked down at the photo. "How do I do this? Do I need to quit my work?"

"No, you don't. We'll take as many precautions with you as we can." Joe was frustrated. He was searching as were others for this man and could not find him. He wanted this over for his friends but it didn't seem as if it would be over any time soon. "Let me have your schedule for each week and we'll work it out."

"My schedule can change from day to day, Joe." Brynne sounded very frustrated. She didn't like how her life was turning out but she had to acknowledge that God was in control and had only the best in mind for her.

—

Joe nodded. He had already been told that by her supervisor. He would work with what he had to the best of his ability. He just knew that she would refuse his help and those of others, just to prove her independence.

Briar opened his mouth and then snapped it closed. He could give them his input but the decision had to be Brynne's. He made a note to himself to talk with her.

Joe finally rose and left, not certain that he had made any impression on Brynne. She was key to solving this mystery and he had no idea how to reach through to her.

—

Chapter 13

Briar paced his office building that next afternoon. He hit the door hard before he strode outside. He was not in the mood to work despite the time constraints that he was working under for that particular fox pelt and form. Briar sighed. He no longer had the interest in the taxidermy world and that had changed when he married Brynne. Briar sighed before he stopped his forward walk and stared up at the sky.

God was here, he knew, and felt His presence surrounding him. He prayed for the peace that he needed in this situation but his emotions were too overwrought at the moment to understand that God was working in his heart and soul and that he would not be left comfortless or alone. Briar turned as he heard footsteps and stared at the man standing near him.

"Can I help you?" Briar didn't move towards the man. Instead, he was ready to run, his muscles tensing as he prepared for that move.

"You're Briar Koyle." The man's words were a statement, not a question. He watched Briar as the younger man simply refused to speak. His hand reached for his identification and he handed it over. "You need to be inside." His hand reached for Briar's arm, shoving him into the building before he slammed the door and locked it after them.

———

Briar spun and stood, hands clenched at his sides, anger on his face. He didn't know this man and had no idea why he had acted as he had.

"Explain yourself and now!" Briar's words bit at the man, waiting impatiently for him to respond.

The man stood with his back against the door, his arms folded across his chest, his brows drawn down as he watched Briar. He had to talk to him. He just didn't know if Briar was in the frame of mind to hear him out.

"Hear me out, Briar." He handed over his identification, this time Briar taking it from him. "I mean you no harm. In fact, we want to work with you to prevent the exportation of animal statues and whatever that may be hidden in them."

"Why?" Briar did not back down from the man. There was too much at stake.

"Why? Because of your work. We know that you have been approached to try and force you to work with them. We know that you were forced to marry without any choice. I was unable to prevent that from happening. We had heard rumours about you and Brynne but we had no idea this was what was planned." He tucked his identification away once more. "We need to speak with Brynne as well, given her line of work."

"Again, why me? I don't understand it." He opened his mouth to call the man by name but hesitated as the man shook his head. "Why Brynne? What did she do to anyone to cause this?"

"She hasn't done anything. Not that we are aware of. Other than being who she is." The man walked away from the door to stare out of one of the windows. "They're out there, waiting for you to come out. You'll disappear, Briar, and not be seen again. You will be forced to do their bidding whether you want to or not." He turned once more to study Briar. "They will use her to get to you."

"They always do that. My brother went through something like this as did some of our friends." Briar stared down at the floor, torn as to what to believe. "How do I know that you are telling me the truth? That you really work for that organization?"

The man nodded. Briar was asking the questions that he should and what he himself would have asked. He tugged a large manila envelope out of his jacket and walked over to drop it onto the desk, watching as Briar moved away from it.

"Read through this. It has my cell number in it. Read it through. Discuss it with Brynne. Then call me." The man unlocked the door and walked away. He was gone from sight before Briar was out of the door and searching for him.

Briar returned to the reception area, standing in front of the desk and staring down at the envelope. He was reluctant to pick it up and walked away from the desk. He headed for his work shop, tidying away what he had been working on. Briar stared at the fox, puzzled as to why the man had wanted.

Grabbing up the envelope, Briar headed for his truck and then home. He was praying for his bride as he did so, begging God to protect her. He parked in his driveway and then ran for the house, unlocking the door and turning off the security system. Briar searched for Brynne, not finding her home as yet. He reached for his phone and didn't see any messages from her. That frightened him. He prayed that she was safe and that God was protecting her. He could do nothing more than that.

Brynne frowned at Briar's truck. He wasn't supposed to be home as of yet. At least, she didn't think that he was. Opening the trunk of her car, she reached for her back pack, shifting it to a shoulder before she reached for the bags of groceries that waited for her. Heading for the kitchen, Brynne set the bags on the table and dropped her back pack on the floor near a counter.

Briar turned from his dresser. He had been changing to more casual clothes and smiled. Brynne was home. He finished dressing rapidly and headed for where he could hear movement. Pausing in the kitchen doorway, Briar watched Brynne for a moment before he was across the room and hugging her.

Brynne gave a brief squeak as she felt arms around her and then was hugging Briar as well. She felt safe again, here in his arms, even though she knew that was far from the case. She had been followed all day as she went about her tasks, even to hearing the snap of twigs breaking not that far from her when she was out in the field. That had scared her more than anything. It had been a spur of the moment decision to go out there that day and she had not had anyone with her.

"Brynne? You're home? Have a good day?" Briar leaned back to look down at her, the ice that had encased his heart melting even more as he studied her face.

"Not really. I was followed all over the place." Brynne's voice was disgruntled. She frowned up at him. "What happened? And don't tell me that nothing did."

"Something did. We need to talk about it and discuss our next steps. First, you were making a meal?"

"Just a salad and cold meat. I hope that is okay." Brynne bit at her lip, unsure if she had chosen correctly to prepare that.

"It's fine, Brynne. That is just fine." Briar dropped a kiss on her forehead before he moved to reach for whatever plates and utensils that they would need.

Brynne stared after him, an astonished look on her face before she shook her head and finished their meal. Seating themselves, Briar reached for Brynne's hand as he prayed for their meal and then for themselves. Brynne stared up at him as he finished before she reached for her fork. This was not what she was used to or expected.

"Briar? You're troubled about something." Brynne refused to wait for their meal to be over before she reached for the large envelope. "What is this?"

"That's what we need to talk about." Briar described the man who had appeared and what he wanted. He frowned. He had not been afraid of the man, just cautious about him. "I have no idea who he was or what organization that he works for. It's supposed to be all in there." He turned as he heard the doorbell. "Were we expecting anyone?"

Brynne shrugged as she was on her feet, heading for the door, stepping back to let Arlyn, Skylor, and Cayce into the house.

"You're all here? What happened?" Brynne immediately assumed that something had.

"Nothing. We just felt a call to be here." Cayce hugged her and headed for the kitchen, his voice greeting his brother.

Arlyn shook his head at Cayce before he took hugged Brynne. She was upset, he knew, and waited for her to speak.

"Brynne? What happened today?" Arlyn watched her carefully, knowing that something had happened that day.

Brynne shrugged, not sure what to say before she walked back into the kitchen. She sat, staring at her food before she pushed the plate away. She no longer had an appetite and only wanted to know what had transpired with her groom that day.

Chapter 14

Skylor sat next to Brynne, studying first the other lady and then Briar. Something had happened that day and she wanted to know exactly what had transpired. She heard the three brothers talking. Skylor frowned. There was an undercurrent in Briar's voice that she had not heard before and that troubled her.

Brynne reached for the envelope and was on her feet, heading away from the kitchen. She dropped in onto Briar's desk before she turned to study the doorway behind her. She shouldn't have done that, she knew, but she also knew that they needed to discuss it between them without letting anyone else know. His family would want to become involved and for once, she had to walk away from them.

Cayce had watched Brynne walk from the kitchen. He hesitated a moment before he followed her, stopping just inside the door. He waited patiently for Brynne to speak. Instead she continued to stare at him.

"Brynne? What happened today?" Cayce kept his voice soft and low. He knew just from experience that he needed to do that.

"What happened today? I was followed. I had to be out in the field and someone was very close to me." Her eyes slid closed as she struggled to control her emotions. She would not cry, she decided, not in front of him.

"And you didn't have anyone with you?" He sighed as Brynne shook her head. "Didn't have time to arrange that?"

"No, I didn't. A situation came up that I had to deal with. Someone reported some injured fox kits. I had to bring them in for treatment." Brynne scowled at him. "I couldn't just leave them there, you know."

"I know, Brynne. Your heart is too tender to do that. And yes, you would go out there on your own. But that's not all." Cayce heard the footsteps that were approaching. He stepped to one side to let the others enter the room.

"No, it wasn't, but it's not my story to tell. Other than that I was followed all day, even when I was in the office." She was sober as she spoke.

"Has Joe searched your office for anything that doesn't belong there?" Arlyn knew that was a possibility, that someone had somehow managed to secrete devices in her office and around her office building. He knew that Briar was searching their home and property daily and was also searching his building.

"I have no idea. He has not been in touch for a few days. Not that I expect him to." Brynne stared at Briar, seeing the compassion on his face and another emotion in his eyes that gave her hope that one day they might really be a couple. She was praying that would happen but really didn't expect it to. Brynne felt unloved and unwanted despite Briar's attempts to prove that she was.

Briar moved past the others to reach for Brynne. She stood stiff in his arms, her eyes on the others

—

despite feeling how hard he was hugging her. Briar sighed. Brynne wasn't responding to him right now and he had no idea how to reach through her.

Arlyn frowned at the couple before his eyes dropped to the envelope. That Brynne was trying to hide it was obvious. He just didn't know why.

"What's that envelope?" Arlyn pushed his brother to answer.

"That? It was handed to me today." Briar sighed. He explained exactly what had happened, his eyes on Brynne as he did so. He saw the fear that was hidden in her eyes and felt her relax suddenly against him.

"What's in it?" Cayce moved to stand at the desk. He didn't touch the envelope, knowing that he couldn't.

"I have no idea." Briar moved away from Brynne to open the envelope and dump out the contents. He was suddenly afraid, afraid for them both and afraid of what the near future would be like. Briar reached for a pen to separate the articles which consisted of a business card, a thumb drive, photos, and other paperwork. He frowned. He didn't know what this meant but someone was serious enough about what they said to do this.

Brynne stared at the business card. She knew that name but she didn't know why. She looked up at Briar, fear running through it. This was much worse than she thought.

—

"That man? Briar! He works for my father." Brynne was almost beside herself. "What did he say?"

"Just that he wanted me to work with him to stop the smuggling." Briar reached for the card, sitting swiftly at his computer and looking for the website. It didn't exist. He thought for a moment before he sent the information on to Blackie, asking that they look into it and bring in anyone who they needed to. He knew that would happen and that they would not be charged for anything.

"Briar?" Skylor had moved to look over the paperwork. "What do we do with this?"

"We look through it and see what we can figure out. Then we talk with Joe." Arlyn reached for the paperwork. "Why would he approach you like that?"

"He wants to find out what all you know." Cayce reached for some of the paperwork, finding a chair to sit before he began to read through what he held in his hands.

Skylor approached Brynne, finding her just standing lost and alone in the centre of the room. She drew her away from the room and to the couch in the living room. Making Brynne sit, Skylor just began to pray for her. Brynne's eyes slid closed as she struggled with her tears. She began to weep, the break in her emotions needed after so many years.

Briar had entered the room, looking for his bride. A soft sound came from him as he saw her tears and he was beside her, wrapping an arm around her. He prayed for her even as he tried to comfort her.

——

Skylor watched them, seeing similarity to what she and Arlyn had gone through. All she could do was share her story once more with Brynne and then pray for her.

Chapter 15

Three days later, Briar looked around from where he was waiting for Brynne to finish work. The man who had appeared at his building was behind him, waiting for him to turn around to face him. Instead, Briar walked into the building and called Joe. He had already spoken to him about the material and the man and then turned over the originals to Joe. Joe had been concerned, especially when he heard who the man was. Briar was pointed towards Brynne's office, the security guard who had been hired walking past him and outside.

The security guard walked towards the man waiting, simply telling him that he needed to leave. The man stared at him, stared past him, and then walked back to his truck. He was frustrated. He was well aware that Brynne had likely figured out who he was. She just didn't know that the organization was real even if they tried to find the website. It would not be found, he knew that much. They used it as a cover and at times it was removed from any internet traffic. That had happened just now, circumstances outside of their control causing that to happen.

Brynne glanced up as Briar found a seat in front of her desk before she was back on the call that she had taken. It lasted far longer than she had wanted. When it was over, Brynne was lost in making her notes before she sat back with a troubled look on her face.

"Brynne? Love? What is it?" Briar spoke quietly, shooting a quick glance over his shoulder. He

———

could hear conversation and footsteps around the office area, knowing that others were around. He caught a glimpse of the security guard pacing the hallway outside of Brynne's office.

"I'm sorry?" Brynne looked up as Briar spoke. She had forgotten that he was there. "Briar? You're here?"

"I am. You're troubled." Briar had no doubt that she was. He knew her well enough now to read the signs even though it had not been that long.

"I am. I need to talk to Jed about what I was told but he's away until next week." Jed was her supervisor. "It's Thursday, isn't it?"

"It is. You're off tomorrow, aren't you?"

"I am." Brynne scowled at him as she answered his question. "Why? You're working?"

"No, I'm not. I finished the fox that I was working on. I don't want to start another one this week. I need to catch up on paperwork but that can wait. You need me." Briar just watched as she studied through his words and her face cleared.

"You are? Then, can we work on whatever it is that we are going through? Brynne was twisting her rings, a nervous habit that she had developed.

"We can. We'll work on it but we're also going out for a meal." Briar was on his feet, reaching for her hand and pulling her to her feet. "Ready to leave?"

"I am." She looked towards the hallway. "The guard's out there?"

—

"He is. The man was back and approached me out in the parking lot. He was chased away, I do believe." Briar grinned at her. "Come on, love. We're going to grab something to take home for our meal."

"That sounds like a plan." Brynne's hand was tight in Briar's as she waved good bye to the rest of the staff, heading out for the parking lot and Briar's truck.

Neither of them saw the man watching them or then following them as they drove to a drive-in restaurant and then through the drive-through to obtain a meal. Briar said afterwards that he felt a tingling on the back of his neck but never paid it any mind. He had not thought of being in danger. Briar's sole focus was on his bride and then praying for God's protection and peace over them. He knew that they were in God's keeping although sometimes it didn't feel that way.

The next morning, Brynne stepped out of the front door and froze in her steps. The man stood there, waiting for the couple. Brynne backed up and slammed the door behind her and locked it before running to find Briar. Briar was only half turned when Brynne hit him, almost knocking them both to the floor.

"Brynne? What happened?" Briar stared down at her and then towards the front door. He tried to move away from her and that didn't happen. Brynne was just not moving and because she was not moving, he couldn't.

"That man? The one who approached you? He's out there on our front walk." Brynne was terrified. All she could do was hold on to Briar and beg God for protection.

Briar finally was able to set Brynne back from him before he stalked towards the front door. He could hear Brynne scurrying after him and felt her hand hit his back, hard. He bent to stare out of the door window. The man had stepped back to the sidewalk but still stood, arms folded on his chest, watching the area around the house. His focus was not on the house itself, Briar could tell. He just didn't want to go out there and confront the man again.

"He's still there, Brynne." Briar stepped back from the door, reaching for his phone. "Let me call Joe and see what he can do for us."

Joe parked down the street from Briar's home and then walked quietly towards the man. He stopped behind him and then reached for the man's wrists, cuffing him and shoving him back to the car and into the back seat. Slamming the door behind him, Joe stared at him and then back towards Briar's home. He sent a simply text message to Briar that he had the man in custody. Could the pair stay out of any other trouble that day?

Brynne stared at the text message, confused at his words.

"Did he really just say that?"

Briar was laughing, knowing that Joe was being facetious.

"He did. He's joking, Brynne. I know that we can't stay out of trouble, not that we're looking for it."

—

83

Briar swung an arm around her and turned her back towards the door. "We're heading out for breakfast. I think that it is safe right now."

"Are you sure?" Brynne scowled at him as he laughed. "I don't think this is very funny."

"It's not but your response is just so you. At least the you that I am coming to know and love." Briar shut the truck door after her, not seeing her shock at his words or the hope that was rising in her eyes.

Chapter 16

Brynne settled herself onto a bench seat in a nearby diner, Briar beside her, before she reached for the menu. She was definitely unsettled that day, and that man was the reason why. She knew that he had been taken into custody but she had no idea for how long. And that terrified her. Anything to do with her family did that to her now.

Briar's hand rested on her hand for a moment before he searched the diner. He could feel someone watching him but the only ones present were town folks. He knew most of them, he thought, before his attention went back to Brynne.

"Brynne? That man? You are sure he's the one who works for your father?" Briar kept his voice low.

"I am. I haven't seen him in years though, just because I wasn't around them." Brynne looked up at him, biting at her lip. She was trying hard to trust in God but He seemed so far away right at the moment.

"God is here, love. He is here with us and is protecting us, whether we know how that is happening. It's hard to trust in times like this." Briar nodded at the server as she brought over mugs of coffee and then took their orders. "We'll pray it through, Brynne. Our family and friends are praying for us."

"Our family? Do you mean your family?" Brynne bit out the words, desperate to belong to Briar's family and didn't think that would even happen.

———

"Our family, Brynne. They are your family. They want desperately to have you accept them but will not push you."

Brynne looked up at him, wonder on her face.

"They want that? I thought that they would hate me, marrying as we did. We still don't know why that happened."

"No, we don't, and we need to find out who is responsible." She looked up as she felt a presence near her and watched Joe slide onto the bench seat across from them. She scowled at him, bringing a grin to his face. "Joe? What did that man want?"

Joe continued to grin at her. He shared a look with Briar who had an answering grin on his face.

"Not yet. We'll talk, Brynne. He's being interrogated even as we speak." Joe sat back, the smile disappearing from his face. "And Briar? I want to know why you've been targeted as you have."

"So would I. How do we do that, Joe? I know how hard it was with Arlyn and Skylor, to figure that out even though we knew her father was involved in some way."

"He was at that. Now, how be we set this aside for now and just enjoy a meal together? I'm sorry. I shouldn't be here." Joe moved to slide away from the couple before Brynne's hand touched his, keeping him in his seat.

"It's okay, Joe. We want you here. Briar and I need you here." She frowned for a moment. "This is not me. I don't say things lie that."

—

"It is you. It's the you that's been hidden for so many years. You're finally free enough from your past to go forward with your life. Briar is helping you to free yourself." Joe smiled gently at his friends. "God is working in your life and bringing that you out of the shadows."

Briar nodded at Joe's words. Just in the few days that he had been married to Brynne, he had seen the change and knew that God was changing him as well.

An hour later, Brynne walked from the diner between the two men. She didn't feel safe but didn't see anyone around who seemed dangerous to her. She turned at that point to say something to Briar. Instead of speaking, her mouth clamped closed as she saw the group that had surrounded them.

Briar had been watching Brynne and had not noticed the group moving in on them. Joe had seen them but had been unable to move the couple to safety. He felt a hand on his arm, shoving him towards a van, hearing Brynne's muttering as the couple were moved that way. The trio were roughly shoved inside, the rolling door slammed down and shutting them into darkness.

Balancing on his feet as the van moved away from the diner, Joe headed for the door, feeling around for any latch that would open it. The swaying of the van prevented him from finding it. He turned in the dark, feeling his way back to where Briar and Brynne had braced themselves.

"Joe? What just happened?" Briar's voice was furious.

"We were just kidnapped. That's what happened. And I would like to know who and why." His phone was out as he called for help, giving a description of the van and what he could remember of the plate number. Joe tucked his phone away. "Someone will be looking for us." He didn't say what he thought. He couldn't. Joe knew that he had been in the wrong place at the wrong time or was it the right place as the right time?

"I get that. But who or why?" Briar had to tamp down his anger. It wasn't helping at this point. He could feel Brynne trembling beside him. He just didn't know whether it was fear or anger causing that to happen. "How many were there?"

"Six that I could see. I'm not sure if anyone was behind the wheel and waiting." Joe was thinking through what had happened before the vibrating of his phone caught his attention. He read the text message and drew in a deep breath. "The officers have stopped the van, Briar, Brynne. Down on the floor and now. Lie flat. And wrap your arms around your heads. We're in a hostage situation right now and I need to make sure that you two are safe. This is one way to do it." Joe was at the back door, on his knees, an ear pressed to the side wall of the van. He could faintly hear the shouts of his fellow officers and the responses of the kidnappers. He could then hear the sound of gunfire and dropped to a prone position on the floor of the van.

Shouts continued to sound through the air before the van took off at a high rate of speed. The three could hear the crunch of vehicles forcefully hit and shoved from the van's path and the resulting yells of the officers and the gunfire that sounded.

Brynne reached for Briar, feeling his arm around her as his head was tight to hers. They were both terrified, not knowing what was happening. The commotion outside of the van had greatly frightened them, not having been in such a situation as before.

Joe crept towards them, a hand out on Briar's back for a moment. The van was swaying widely as it sped from the officers. The sirens from the pursuing vehicles sounded faintly through the walls of the van. A sudden jolt caused the van to sway even wilder before it tipped to one side and hovered on two wheels before it landed back on its four wheels. The three in the back of it were tossed with the movement of the van and lay motionlessly as the vehicle came to a halt.

Chapter 17

More sirens and emergency lights split the morning air and sky as they raced to the scene of the accident. The officers were reaching for the men in the front of the van, withdrawing their hands as they realized that the men were dead. Their attention then turned to the back of the van. They were unable to raise the door, having to wait for the firefighters to wrench open the door and raise it to allow access to the three inside.

The firefighters struggled to tear away the door, fighting the damage done as the van had rolled. They finally were able to cut through the metal and drag it away, allowing access for the paramedics. These emergency personnel were inside the van and assessing the three, calling for backboards, neck collars, and stretchers. They worked frantically to stabilize the trio before they were transported to the paramedic rigs and the rigs racing away, full siren and emergency lights in force. Patrol vehicles cut through traffic to clear a path for the speeding vehicles.

The activity around the van didn't slow at all as the investigation continued and the coroner arrived. It would have continued anyway but with a fellow officer involved, it took on an intensity that was obvious to even the most oblivious onlooker.

Ardan stood back from his front door, shock on his face as an officer entered. To hear that both Briar and Brynne had been kidnapped and then injured was not how he expect to start his Friday. He reached for

---

Bessie and ran for his car, Bessie's phone in her hand as she sent out a group text asking the others in the family to meet them at the hospital.

Officers surrounded the group as they waited impatiently and with worry in their hearts for word on the couple. To hear that Joe had been involved was a surprise to them as well. They prayed for the three, begging God to spare their lives and heal them. They prayed as well for protection of the trio, knowing that they would be under protective security as they were assessed.

The physicians stood back, shock on their faces. These three should not be alive. As they were alive, they should have been seriously injured if not in life-threatening condition. They shared looks as the trio were each taken for imaging studies and then returned to the examination rooms. They were in awe of their conditions, knowing that only One had been responsible for that and that One was God.

Ardan was on his feet as he saw a nurse approaching them and reached for Bessie's hand. Arlyn stood with Skylor tucked tight to him, Cayce and Anna beside them, as the older couple disappeared. They shared a look, something that they seemed to be doing a lot of lately.

Ardan and Bessie paused in the doorway to the room where their son lay. They could see him from where they stood. The physician turned from the stretcher and beckoned them forward.

"Ardan? Bessie? Your son is indeed a fortunate man. God had His hand on him. He is battered and

---

bruised. He does have a broken collar bone which will affect his work. However it could have been much worse."

Bessie's hand was on her son's head, praising God for the good news. She frowned and then turned to the physician.

"Brynne? Briar's wife?"

"Brynne? Another physician is treating her. If you wish to come with me, I'll find someone to bring Anna and the other boys back to be with Briar."

The older couple listened at the physician described Brynne's injuries, which included a probable concussion and multiple bruises and scrapes. The physician was amazed as well that she had not been hurt worse than she was.

Joe was awake and somewhat alert three hours after the accident. He was refusing to remain in the hospital and was on his feet, hunting for Briar and then Brynne. He stood at their bedsides for a moment before he turned and headed for the outside, officers surrounding him as he did so.

Early that afternoon, Briar walked away from the hospital, sore and hurting, with Brynne at his side. They didn't wait for anyone to come for them to give them a lift to their home. Briar had sent out a text message to his family that they were heading home and that they would meet with them the next afternoon. They both needed to sleep but they didn't want to. They wanted to find the men who were after them instead.

—

Brynne yawned as she dressed in clean clothes. She was exhausted and hurting in so many ways. She looked longingly at her bed before she headed for the kitchen. Briar was waiting for her, his arm out to draw her close to him. She hugged him, being mindful of his sling.

"Briar? How can you work?"

"I won't be. I'll go through what I have to do and contact the clients. I'm sure that it will be okay." Briar swayed for a moment before Brynne was pulling out a chair and gently pushing him down into it. "Thank you. You're okay?"

Brynne shrugged. She didn't know if she was or wasn't.

"I'm tired, Briar. I need to sleep but I need to watch out for you." Brynne was downcast, not her usual self. She reached for their coffee mugs and set them down on the table before she sat beside him, her chair as close to Briar's as she could.

"Can we pray, Briar? And what about Joe?"

"Joe's at work. He shouldn't be but he's mad and wants to know who did this. And yes, we need to pray. God is the only one Who will get us through this all. Joe said he'd check in with us later today."

"I don't understand what happened." Brynne sighed as her head went down against his good shoulder.

Briar gave a thoughtful smile, his heart hurting for his bride. He didn't know where this would end or even when. All he knew was that he had to pray for them and pray hard, even though others were praying for them. They had to personally commit themselves to God and His protection.

Chapter 18

Dressed for bed that evening, Brynne walked through their home, finally realizing that she was home. She had never felt like that at her own place. She sighed. It needed to be cleared out so that she could give it back to the landlord. He had told her to take her time.

Brynne paused at Briar's open bedroom doorway, watching as he tossed restlessly. He had taken the pain medications that she had held out for him, a disgruntled look on his face mingling with the pain. Without thinking, Brynne walked towards the bed and sat, a hand on his head. Briar stopped moving, a soft thank you from him. Brynne was torn as to what to do before she was on her feet and walking away, trouble on her face.

The next morning, Cayce locked the door behind him, frowning at Brynne. She looked rough, he decided, as if she had not slept.

"Brynne?" Cayce's words stopped her.

"What?" Brynne snapped at Cayce before she walked away. She had not slept much the night before, watching over Briar as she had. She folded the blanket that she had been holding when she answered the door and let Cayce in.

Cayce shook his head before he went looking for Briar, finding his brother sitting on the side of the bed. He sat beside him, waiting for Briar to speak. He prayed for his brother and his wife, knowing that God would be the One Who would lead to the solution and protection for them.

"Thanks, Cayce." Briar's voice was rough with an early morning roughness.

"For what?" Cayce was puzzled, not sure what Briar was saying.

"For helping me during the night." Briar turned his head carefully to stare at his brother, seeing the blank look on his face. "You were here, right?"

"No, I wasn't. I just got here."

"Then, who helped me up and down over the night?" Briar's eyes closed. "Brynne."

"It would have been Brynne. She looks as if she hasn't slept." Cayce helped his brother to his feet and then to dress before the two men headed for the kitchen.

Briar paused as he saw Brynne just sitting at the table, her head buried on her folded arms. He rested a hand on her head before she was pulled to her feet and with an arm around her, Briar guided her to her bedroom and then covered her with a blanket as she slept. He stood for a moment, praying for his bride before he turned, slightly unsteady on his feet.

Cayce was waiting for his brother as were their parents. Ardan and Bessie had shown up, Cayce quietly letting them into the house. Bessie moved past the men to find Brynne, the bedroom door closed quietly behind her. Ardan in turn reached for his son, turning him towards his office and a seat there. He crouched beside the chair, watching Briar closely.

—

"Son?" Ardan was highly worried about his middle son. It had been hard enough with that Arlyn had gone through. They had all prayed that Briar and Cayce would be spared, but it seemed as if that would not happen. God was still in control and all Ardan could do was pray for peace in the situation.

"Dad? You're here?" Briar raised his head, grimacing with pain as his shoulder moved. His hand rested on the upper arm on that side of his body.

"We're here, son. Do you want anything?" Ardan looked around as Cayce appeared with a tray in his hands. "Here's Cayce with some toast for you. You do need to eat."

"I do." Briar looked around. "Where's Brynne?"

"She's sleeping, son. Mom's looking after her." Ardan rose to his feet, watching his son closely. He sighed and walked away, his phone out to call Joe. "Joe? How are you feeling?"

"Not great." Joe stood from his office desk, walking towards the break room. "Where are you?"

"With Briar and Brynne. What can you tell them?"

"Not a lot right now. I'll stop by this afternoon." Joe tucked his phone away, intent on the investigations that were open on his desk. He couldn't spend all his time on Briar's case as much as he wanted to. That he had become a participant in it had never crossed his mind. Another investigator had taken on that part of the case.

Brynne was on her feet a couple of hours later, reaching for clean clothes. She frowned. She didn't remember coming to her room or even sleeping, but it seemed that she had. She paused for a moment to bow her head before her God and then opened the door. Faint conversation reached Brynne's ears from the office. She turned instead to the kitchen, needing to eat and find something to drink.

Skylor looked around as Brynne appeared.

"Brynne? Looking for food?" Skylor grinned at the other lady.

"I am. I need to. Where's the investigation standing?" Brynne sipped at the mug of tea that she had been handed.

"About there. Blackie and his friend, Simon, are here. They're pulling in other friends as well. They want this over for you and Briar."

Brynne nodded, knowing that was the truth. She turned away from Skylor and headed for the office, standing outside of the room and watching the activity inside. Brynne than walked away and headed for the back deck. She found the seat that she preferred and sank into it. The sounds of the afternoon nature sounded in her ears. Her eyes closed as she wept, the years of being beaten down and neglected too much for her heart to bear.

Briar had risen as he heard the soft footsteps outside of the office. He followed her, nodding at Skylor as he passed her. He stood on the back deck before he was across to the love seat and wrapping an arm around his bride as he sat beside her. His own

—

tears wet her hair as he wept for her, not sure why she was weeping. It had all become just too much for him.

Brynne jumped as she felt his arm around her, turning against him. She finally stopped weeping, content to be held. She heard his prayers for them, sprinkled with verses of God's protection, His help, and petition for His peace in all of this. Brynne knew that God was the only one Who could give them peace. That had been proven over the years in her own life.

—

Chapter 19

Late that evening, Brynne walked around outside of the house, looking for anything that was out of order. Briar had already retired, the pain medications much needed but also very much making him drowsy. She turned as she heard footsteps approaching her and backed away from the man. She didn't know him.

"Who are you?" Brynne's voice was tight and fear-filled.

"I don't mean you any harm, Brynne." He pulled out a wallet from his pocket and held it out to you. "My name's Will. I work undercover in the downtown area." He then took back his wallet and pocketed it. He pulled out a long white envelope and extended it to her, waiting for her to take it. "It won't bite you, Brynne." He grinned at her. "In fact, it might just help you solve this." Will walked away at that, disappearing from sight.

Brynne stared after him before she stared down at the envelope. She had not been frightened, and that surprised her. She made her way back into the house, locking the doors behind her and then finding Briar. Brynne stared down at him before she simply laid down beside him, cuddling close to find comfort and protection from him even though he was not able to protect her as he would have liked to have.

Briar roused slightly before his arm moved to cuddle her close to him. He slept once more, content to know that Brynne was safe. They didn't realize that things were about to get much worse for them and it would only be God who would protect them and bring through the floods and fires of destruction and defeat to stand triumphant in His power.

Briar stared down at the envelope on the kitchen table. Brynne was still sleeping and he had no inclination to awaken her. He reached for it and opened it, surprised at what he was reading. This couldn't be right, he decided, before he was heading for his office, a hand holding the letter and holding his upper arm at the same time. Briar was hurting that Sunday morning, knowing that they needed to be in church but also knowing that he would not push Brynne if she wasn't up to the scrutiny that would inevitably be directed their way.

Sitting at his desk, Briar hesitated to open the letter. Brynne must have found it at some point yesterday after he had slept. His head turned as he studied the door. He had not expected to find her cuddling up to him but that was okay in his books. Brynne was working her way into his heart and he didn't want her to walk away from him, ever.

Instead of reaching for the letter, Briar's head bowed. He spent time just sitting in silence before God, knowing that he had to be silent to understand God's peace. He needed that peace going forward. His thoughts then turned to God's protection and how that was provided. Briar acknowledged that God was the only One who could and would protect them. He knew from Arlyn that it would be difficult to keep that faith but that God was faithful to them. They just might not like what they would go through.

———

A hand on his good shoulder roused him at last, turning his face towards Brynne. His arm came out to wrap around her and draw her close to him. He was in love with his bride and prayed that she would feel the same about him.

"Where did you find the letter?" Briar reached for the envelope.

"Someone named Will left it for us. He showed me his badge." Brynne was troubled by that.

"He's undercover. He and someone named Bob helped Skylor." Briar opened the letter and unfolded the pages. "He's provided a lot of information for us."

"He has." Brynne looked over at the clock. "It's almost time for church, Briar. Are you up to it?"

Briar shrugged. It was really up to Brynne whether they went or not.

"We can watch online this morning, if you prefer. We're still pretty sore from Friday."

"We are and that works." Brynne didn't move, content to stand next to Briar, her arm on his good shoulder. "Briar, we need to talk."

"And we will. For now, let's find our seats for church and then spend some time in prayer." He looked at the unfolded papers. "This can wait."

"It can. It can wait forever, as far as I'm concerned." Brynne walked away, heading for the kitchen to retrieve two bottles of water. She turned to find Briar behind her, a troubled look on his face. "Briar? It's true. I want this over and it just isn't. No one has enough information to stop what is happening."

"No, we don't. Every little piece that we find or someone else finds works towards that goal. I don't know why God is allowing this other than to bring someone to justice."

"And that's what is happening. It's hard to understand. How do we have mercy on whoever it is? I can't extend mercy towards my family, not on my own. God is working in my heart to extend His mercy to them. I just don't want to give up my anger and whatever other emotion that I'm feeling towards them." Brynne's face was sober as she spoke. She knew that she was not showing disrespect for her Heavenly Father. She was just working through the struggles of what He was asking of her.

"It's hard, love. It's very hard. We'll pray that way for you. It is hard to forgive someone who has treated you that way. But God is here. He is working in this situation. He will protect us, even though we don't like how that protection works."

"That's what I don't understand." Brynne twisted the bottle of water in her hands. "I just don't understand that."

"There are things that we will never understand here on earth, Brynne. It's just how it is. God has a bigger plan than we do. A friend tells me that God has plans and purposes for us that we don't know and may never know."

"I get that as well." Brynne was sober. "I hate that you have been hurt and that Joe was hurt. It shouldn't have happened."

"It does happen, no matter how careful we are. For now, let's set it aside. Blackie and Simon have information, he tells me, that they want to share with us. Later this week." Briar stared down at his sling. "It's not like I'll be working."

"I called my boss and took a leave of absence. The men have been inside the building. I feel that it is too dangerous for my fellow workers if I'm there." Brynne was sober and saddened at that. "I don't want any of them hurt because of me."

"That's likely a good idea." Briar shifted his weight, his eyes closing against the pain as he did so. He was reluctant to move and felt that Brynne felt the same.

Chapter 20

Joe walked slowly towards Briar as he stood outside of his building on the Monday morning. He was moving slower than he had been the day before. He hurt in places he didn't think could hurt.

Briar had turned as he heard the car motor, an arm tightening around Brynne as he did so. She was frowning at Joe as well, trying to determine just why he was there. She sighed. Joe needed to be off work and wouldn't take the time, not while he had so many investigations to solve. Theirs was just one of them.

"Joe? What are you doing here?" Briar finally spoke. He turned to open the building door before entering.

Brynne headed for the mail that had been dropped through the mail slot and dropped it onto the reception desk. She would look it over in a while. For now, she too wanted to know why Joe was there.

"I just needed to see how you two are." Joe slumped into a chair, his eyes closing for a moment. He looked up at Briar who stood over him. "Briar? Will told me that he had been in touch."

"He has been." Briar sighed and then pulled out his phone. "I'll send you copies of what he provided. I don't like the inferences that he's making."

Joe nodded, his phone out so that he could read through what Will had provided. He looked thoughtful as he finished before he was reading it over once more. "Briar, what are your thoughts?"

"My thoughts?" Briar rubbed at his temple with a forefinger. "I don't know what to say. I have no idea who those people are that he's named."

"And I don't either." Brynne spoke without looking up from where she was working on the mail. "And who are they, any way?"

"I don't know. I will certainly be looking into them." Joe sighed, the headache he was fighting not easing at all. "How are you two?"

"We're hurting, Joe, in more ways than one." Brynne finally looked at the detective. "Briar can't work and he needs to. It will be a while before he can. They're talking surgery for the collar bone if it doesn't heal. I've taken a leave from the work I love just because I don't feel that my fellow workers are safe at all right now." She folded her hands on top of the pile of mail. "And we're hurting physically and emotionally. We were forced to marry when we didn't know one another. That's not how it should have been."

Joe was nodding. He had a good idea that was how they were feeling. He had spent time that morning in counsel with their pastor, trying to understand what was happening and his reactions to the adventure that seemed to be sucking him into its depth, no matter how he tried to stay professional and on track to solve it.

"What information can you share with me that you're trying your best to hide, Brynne?" Joe was on his feet, sorting through the paperwork and taking pictures of the pages. "When did you get this?"

"Yesterday. We've read it over and think we know what it going on. But we can't be sure. I have forwarded copies on to Blackie and Simon. They are planning on being here in the next couple of days." Briar was exhausted and found a chair to seat once more, his pacing causing Brynne to frown at him.

"They are? That's good." Joe was quiet as he read through the material. "Brynne? Do you know these men and women who are named?"

Brynne shook her head and then realized that Joe was not looking at her. She stared past him at the soft sage walls and dark trim. She opened her mouth and then snapped it closed. Brynne was torn. She didn't know them off hand, she could honestly say, but that didn't mean the people didn't work for her father.

"I don't know them. But if they had nothing to do with the house or grounds, I wouldn't have met them. It's entirely possible what Will has said." Brynne buried her head in the arms that she had folded on the desk top. Her voice was muffled as she continued. "Is he going to haunt every step I take? I don't understand how a father could do this. Or a mother either. She's just as guilty as he is."

"We know that, Brynne. Now, I need you to give me a list of all your relatives. We have to look into them as well." Joe was not surprised as Brynne waved a paper at him without looking at him. "You're ahead of me."

"Briar suggested it. It's what you need to do, isn't it?" Brynne looked up at that before she was on her feet and heading out of the office and deeper into the building.

Briar was on his feet, following her. Joe could hear their quiet conversation before Briar returned to find his seat once more.

"Briar? What are your thoughts?" Joe waited patiently for his friend to speak.

Briar shrugged. He had no idea what to think. Right now, he felt in too much pain to think through anything at that point. Briar looked towards the door to his work room, knowing that he needed to be in there but couldn't.

"That's fair, Briar. It's about what I would expect you to not say." Joe finally rose and walked away, needing to be somewhere else. There were just so many crimes happening right at the moment.

Briar was on his feet at last and headed into his work room. Brynne was there, wandering around it and trying to understand just what Briar exactly did. She paused at the fox that he had just finished, a hand touching one of its ears. She jumped as she felt an arm around her.

"This is beautiful, Briar. It is just so natural as it's looking down at the ground. I think I can hear the mouse hiding from it." Brynne carefully leant back against him.

"That's what I was aiming for. There is just something about nature that is soothing and peaceful. I mean, I know that it can seem violent at times but that is how life works." Briar shifted to look around the room. "I have things that I need to do and can't." He was sober and saddened at that.

"And it's all my fault." Brynne was convinced of that no matter what anyone said to her.

"No, it's not. It's the fault of whoever it is that is behind these." Briar prayed for his bride and then for those who were involved in their adventure.

Chapter 21

Arlyn carefully shut the building door behind him a couple of hours later, searching for his brother. His heart had troubled him to the point that he had to find him. He walked through to the work room, standing just inside the door and listening to the conversation between Briar and Brynne. It was somewhat heated, he could tell.

Brynne looked past Briar, jumping in fear until she recognized Arlyn.

"Arlyn? Talk to your brother. Let him know that he can't work." Brynne's voice was full of remorse or whatever emotion that she was feeling at the moment.

"He'll find some way to do that. How be we set that aside from the moment?" Arlyn held up a bag of food. "I brought some food for us." Arlyn stared at his brother who had turned to face him, a slight shake of his head.

"That sounds good." Briar watched as Brynne took the food and walked away, a defeated slump to her shoulders. "She's hurting, Arlyn. How do I help her?"

"By being there for her. Praying for her. Talking everything over with her. It's different for you and Brynne. You're married and can be together all the time. I couldn't do that with Skylor." He frowned at his brother. "Josh and Leah would be good to talk with. They married not long after they met." His face lit up. "And then there's Baird and Berneen and others of the Barnabas Foundation. We need to take a road trip over three.”

Briar blinked at his brother and then his face lit up.

“We do. It would help Brynne a lot.” Briar looked around his shop. “Brynne has this idea that she can help me in here, such as holding a pelt as I work on it. That might just help me to manage.”

“That would work. You’re hurting, brother. What’s the word on the shoulder?”

Briar shrugged as best as he could. He had spoken with the surgeon earlier and had been told that the bone should heal on its own. At the time, he had not been told that it was not a complete break but just a partial one. That made it much better for healing. Briar said as much to his brother.

“That’s an answer to prayer. Now, let’s eat and then see what we can do for you.” Arlyn grinned at his brother. “I can set aside my research for the day if that helps.”

“It should.”

Late that afternoon, Joe turned from the crime scene that he had been working. Will and Bob stood nearby, waiting for him to be free to speak with them.

“Will? Bob? What’s going on?” Joe walked towards them. “How be we grab a meal?”

Will and Bob nodded, following Joe into a local cafe to find seats in a booth. They waited as their meal orders were taken before they glanced at one another.

———

"What is going on with Briar?" Bob spoke for the duo.

"About that. Why do you ask?" Joe waited for them to speak.

"We're hearing rumours on the street about them. Will approached Brynne earlier." Bob frowned at Joe as he nodded. "You have the information."

"I do." Joe responded to Bob's simple statement. "I got it earlier from them. I just don't understand it, though."

"That's what is puzzling us. We don't know who or why. Or do we?" Will frowned at his food, not sure if he wanted to eat or not.

"Brynne has stated that she doesn't recognize any of the names, but she also said that if they weren't involved in the house, she wouldn't have known them. That just adds to what we need to do." Joe rubbed at his forehead. "Have you come across anything else?"

"No, we haven't. We are looking." Bob was on his feet, walking away, leaving Will to stare after him.

"He's upset, Joe. He's been watching out for Brynne for years. They were in public school together before they went their separate ways in high school. He's worried that she'll be hurt worse."

"They were? I didn't know that." Joe was lost in thought for a moment before his notebook was out and he was jotting down his thoughts. "Thanks, Will. That information may be helpful."

Brynne watched Briar closely, seeing how his face was whiter than it should have been. She was worried about him and didn't know how to express herself without sounding as if she wanted to run his life. That was not true at all.

Briar turned at last, his hand rubbing at his shoulder and collar bone area. He needed to go home but didn't want to. He wanted to work on the pelt that was next in line but he couldn't. Briar looked up at Brynne and then walked towards her.

"Ready to go?" Briar reached to lock the door after them.

"I am." Brynne studied the area around them. "Someone is out there, Briar."

"There is. There always is. Come on, love. Let's head for home." Briar's stride was slow, aching as he was from his experience.

Brynne watched him closely, seeing the pain that he was trying to hide. She sighed. He would not slow down, she knew, but would continue to push himself until he collapsed. And Brynne was afraid that the men out there would overtake them and harm him even more than they had.

Briar walked through his yards that night, eyeing everything. Something felt off, he decided, but he had no idea what it was. He would call Joe in the morning, he decided, before he headed back to the house to find Brynne waiting for him, her arms wrapped around her abdomen. Briar decided that he liked having her waiting for him very much and reached to hug her.

———

Chapter 22

The next morning, Briar walked back through his yards, this time Brynne pacing beside him. He frowned as he looked around. Something was off, he once more decided. He just didn't know what.

Brynne looked around as well, trying to determine just what Briar was up to. She walked away from him, studying the gardens. They needed to be worked in and Briar had told her just to go ahead with do what she wanted to. He hadn't done much with them other than weeding them and trimming back what needed to be trimmed.

Looking at the object in the one garden, Brynne backed away quickly, hitting Briar as she did so. His arm wrapped around her to help her stay on her feet. He frowned as he stared at her and then at the garden.

"Brynne? What's in there?" Briar stepped past her to stare down at the package lying there. "What is this?"

"I have no idea and I don't want to know." Brynne moved away, her phone out as she called for Joe to come and take that package away.

Joe had stared at his phone and then responded that he would be there shortly. Were they in danger, he asked? He grinned as Brynne responded that she had no idea if they were in danger or not. Wasn't that his job to decide that?

Joe grinned to himself as he listened to her words. Yes, it was his job to decide that, but he also was enough of a realist to know that they were in danger and Brynne was well aware of that. She was just deflecting her anger towards him and he could take that.

Staring at the package as a crime scene tech stood at his side, Joe shook his head. He had no idea what this was. He walked back towards where the couple were waiting for him. Joe was suddenly very much afraid for them.

"Joe? What is it?" Brynne questioned him before he had even reached them.

"I have no idea as of yet, Brynne. Talk to me about it." Brynne scowled at him. She sighed and then turned and walked back into the house.

The two men watched her walk away before Briar spoke.

"She's worried, Joe, and I would like to relieve that worry if I could."

"I know that she is. She's not acting as she had been. She's found freedom with you that she never had and her emotions are all over the place. God is working in her life, I can see that just in the few days that you two have been together."

"He is. She's questioning everything right now and rightly so. We have been talking about what we're going through and what God is doing for us. It's hard to accept that He only wants the best for us in whatever we are going through. It's tough to understand something like that."

"It is. You know that from Arlyn and Skylor." Joe turned slightly to watch the activity in the garden. "Go on in with Brynne, Briar. I'll come in shortly or as shortly as I can. I need to find out what was in that package. Have you received anything else?"

Briar shook his head. He had turned everything over to Joe all the while keeping a copy for them to go over. He walked into the house, not finding Brynne. Searching for her, he found her in the office, her Bible on her knee, her head bowed over it. He sat beside her, his arm around her, waiting as she struggled with her emotions.

"Where is God, Briar?" Brynne didn't look up. Her emotions were that raw, she was afraid to do so.

"He's here, Brynne. He's right here with us. He never leaves us alone. He is protecting us all the time, whether we feel that or not. He calms the storm around us and within us. He wants only the best for us. God has plans and purposes for us that we don't know about."

"Where does mercy come in?" Brynne looked up, a bleak look on her face. "Do I need to extend mercy to my family? I'm not sure that I can do that."

"On your own, you can't. With God, you can. You can forgive them for what they did. God wants that for you." Briar's arm tightened around her as he dropped a kiss on her cheek. "We'll work it through together." He looked around as he heard footsteps and Arlyn and Cayce appeared. "You two are here?"

"We are. We felt that we had to be. What's going on with the back yard?" Arlyn found a seat near his brother.

"Brynne found a package in the yard and called in Joe. We don't know what is in it. Joe has not said as of yet." Briar was highly worried about Brynne and what was in that package. Joe had not appeared in the house even though Briar had paced back to the door and then back to where Brynne was.

"A package? You're starting to get those now?" Cayce shook his head. "Why doesn't that surprise me?" He looked around, seeing Brynne watching him, a shuttered look on her face. "Brynne? What are your thoughts?"

"My thoughts? I have no idea what to think or say." Brynne brushed past the men, her bedroom door closing quietly behind her.

The brothers shared a look before Briar stepped out into the hallway to stare at the closed bedroom door. Staring at the door, he drew in a deep breath, feeling the pain from his collar bone. He turned then to his brothers, determination on his face.

"How do we do this? How do we find the ones after her?" Briar's face was shuttered for a moment. He hadn't said anything to his brothers but he was deeply in love with Brynne at this point. That was something that he and Brynne were speaking and talking about. It was too new and too fresh to share with anyone.

The two other brothers shared a look before Arlyn shook his head and headed for the back deck.

He stood and watched the activity in the back yard, seeing Joe glancing at him and the turning back to his investigation. Arlyn sighed. This was not what they had expected to find that day when they arrived, but he decided that they should have.

Chapter 23

Brynne ran for the house two days later, hearing the pounding footsteps behind her. She wrenched the door open and then slammed it shut, shoving the lock on and then dropping to the floor. Her back was against the door. She could feel it shaking and then the pounding on it as the man who had chased her through the yard tried to enter. Brynne buried her face against her upraised knees, the denim rough on her face. She refused to move even as the man gave up at last and disappeared.

Briar entered the house by the front door hours later. He frowned as he didn't hear any sound from Brynne. That was unusual. If she was at home when he returned, she came to find him. He headed for his office to drop his briefcase on his desk, a hand rubbing at his shoulder. It was paining him that day, and it was exhausting them.

Searching through the house, Briar stopped in the hallway outside of the bedroom. He couldn't see his bride. He turned to head for the kitchen, stopping in shock and then fear as he almost ran across the room to drop to his knees beside her. Wrapping Brynne into his arm, he tried to raise her to her feet. She just didn't move and he couldn't pick her up. Giving up at last, Briar simply sat beside her, keeping her wrapped tight to him.

Afterwards, Briar had no idea how long that they had sat on the floor. He also had no idea how long Brynne had been huddled against the door. She just wasn't responding to him. Briar could only pray for her.

Rising as he heard pounding at his front door, Briar staggered for a moment as the blood returned to his lower limbs. He stared down at Brynne before he walked towards the door, opening it without thinking. A sudden blow to his injured shoulder sent him back against the wall, a cry of pain drawn from him. He looked at the men who had stormed into his home, his eyes blurred from the pain that the blow had caused. Briar tried to straighten back up but a hand on his injured shoulder kept him in place.

The men remained silent even as one of them walked through the house, standing over Brynne. He smirked an evil smile as he reached for her hair to yank her head back. He stared at her before he shoved her head back down and walked away from her. The man earlier in the day had done what was needed to be done. Brynne had frozen in fear and that was exactly what they wanted.

The men still didn't speak as a blow was landed once more on Briar's injured shoulder. The pain sent him to his knees, his arms tightly grasped in the men's hands. His head dropped as he tried to breathe through the pain. Briar vaguely heard the words spit at him in anger but afterwards, he could not tell anyone what they were. He dropped to lie flat on the floor, his consciousness fading at the men walked away, the front door swinging slightly in the breeze. The men just didn't bother to close it.

Early that evening, Cayce parked his truck in front of his brother's home. He frowned as he felt evil nearby. He just couldn't see anyone who seemed to be that person. Cayce waved at the neighbour across the street who was working in his yard before he turned to the house. He frowned. Something seemed off about it, but he just couldn't decide what it was.

Stopping at the bottom of the front steps, Cayce stared at the open door. He frowned. This was not Briar to do this at any time, especially not with what was he and Brynne were going through. He rapidly climbed the few steps, his fingers out to touch the door and gently shove it open. He called for Briar before his eyes dropped to the floor. A cry was torn from his body as he dropped to his knees beside his brother. Briar didn't respond and didn't move from where he was crumpled on the floor, his good hand dangling over his chest. Cayce reached for his wrist, his head falling forward as he drew in a deep breath of relief. Briar was still alive even though it looked as if he wasn't.

Cayce pulled out his phone to call for the emergency services that were required. A sudden thought had him on his feet and searching the house before he stopped abruptly in front of Brynne. Once more, he reached for a wrist, once more drawing in a breath of relief.

He stood back as the emergency personnel moved in. Cayce rubbed at his neck, not sure where to go or what to say. He walked from the house, finding Joe waiting for him.

"Cayce? What did you see?" Joe drew him off to one side.

"What did I see? An open door. Briar on the floor unconscious. And Brynne the same in the kitchen. I saw no one. I could feel evil out here when I arrived. His neighbour was outside doing yard work when I got here. I waved at him before I headed for the house." Cayce was more than a little worried about his brother and his bride. "There was no signs anywhere, Joe. Not that I could see."

"I see. Stay at your truck, Cayce. I'll have someone drive you to the hospital." Joe paused, a hand rubbing at his phone. "Call your folks and have them meet you at the hospital. They'll be transporting Briar and Brynne shortly."

Cayce nodded, returning to lean against his truck, his eyes on the house. All he could do was pray for his family, knowing that it would be a while before they would hear anything about the couple. Cayce was refusing to leave, not that he could any way. His truck was now behind police lines and he would not be able to drive it away to follow the ambulances when they left.

His phone chiming with a text message startled him for a moment. Cayce reached for it, squinting at the screen in the bright sunlight. A hand cupped around the screen helped him to focus on it, or as focus on it as best he could. Cayce glanced up at the house, not seeing his brother or Brynne being brought out yet. They were alive, he knew, but just what their condition was? That was a different story. Cayce fully believed that God was in control. It just seemed that sometimes God was distant in a situation, and this was one of those times.

Turning back to his phone, Cayce sighed. His mother was looking for Briar and Brynne. They had planned on meeting for supper that night and they hadn't appeared. Did he know where they were? Cayce knew exactly where they were and he was so afraid for them. He sent a simple text back to his mother, stating that something had happened to the couple. He didn't have any information to tell them other than that they would need to meet at the hospital. Cayce tucked his phone away once more into his pocket despite the chiming of multiple text message notifications. He couldn't concentrate on them at the moment. The paramedics were bringing out the two stretchers. Cayce walked rapidly towards the one that held Briar, hopping up into the paramedic rig and settling himself into a corner.

Joe watched him, shaking his head. Cayce really shouldn't have done that, but he didn't have the heart to stop him. He turned back to the investigation, not finding any evidence that would tell him what had happened.

Chapter 24

Cayce turned as he heard rapid footsteps approaching him. His mother wrapped him into a hug before stepping back and letting Ardan do the same. He could see his aunt standing nearby and Arlyn and Skylor almost running towards him. Cayce had found a seat in the waiting room, knowing that he couldn't be back with Briar, no matter how much he wanted to be there.

"Son? What can you tell us?" Ardan spoke for the group.

"Not a lot, Dad. I went to find them. Briar was unconscious in the entry way. The door was open, which is not him. Not at this time. I looked for Brynne and found her sitting against the back door. She just didn't respond to me. I don't know what happened." Cayce was distraught at that. "Joe was there but he didn't talk to me other than to ask me what I found." Cayce paced away from his family, Arlyn at his side.

"Cayce? What are your thoughts?" Arlyn spoke at last. "What did you see?"

"Nothing, Arlyn. Absolutely nothing." Cayce spun to stare at his family who had found seats near the door. "I don't understand what happened. How do we find out?"

"We wait for Briar to wake up." Arlyn chewed at his lower lip, an arm out to wrap around Skylor as she approached him. "Skylor? What are you thinking?"

Skylor stared at the doors to the examination rooms. She shrugged, not sure what to think any more. She knew what she had felt like when she and Arlyn had gone through.

"I think that she may be giving up. We talked yesterday. She said that she was really discouraged at what was happening and that she just didn't think that she could cope any more." Skylor had prayed with Brynne and shared many verses and thoughts about God's protection. "Given how her family treated her, I can understand to some degree how she feels." She leaned against Arlyn, feeling comfort from his hug.

"Is that so?" Cayce nodded. "I can see that. I think that was the thought that I had when I found her. She just seemed so out of it." He walked towards his parents who were on their feet as a nurse approached them.

Bessie and Ardan hesitated before they approached Briar's bed. He was still unconscious, with deep lines of pain etched on his face. Bessie reached to touch her son's hair, more than worried about him. Ardan's hand rested on his son's good shoulder. Cayce stood at the end of the bed for a moment before he walked away to find Brynne.

Brynne was still unconscious as well. The nurses and physician were puzzled by that. She had no obvious signs of injuries and her blood work had come back clear. She was not injured or drugged in any manner. Cayce stood and watched Brynne for a moment before he walked back to find Arlyn and Skylor.

"Brynne needs someone with her, preferably a female. Skylor? She needs you and Aunt Anna." Cayce watched as the two ladies walked away. "Arlyn? Briar is still not awake but he looks as if he is in a lot of pain. Brynne is still out of it. They don't know why though."

"We'll get it figured out." Arlyn turned as he felt a presence beside him. "Joe? What can you tell us?"

Joe shook his head. He had no idea what had happened until he spoke with Briar and Brynne. From what he was told, that would be a while. He sighed to himself before he walked away, heading for his car and another crime scene. There just seemed to be too many right now.

Arlyn and Cayce shared a look before they slumped into seats. They would go back when they could but for now, they would wait and pray. They watched the foot traffic around them, nodding at friends and acquaintances who passed by them.

An hour later, Bessie came looking for her sons. She sat between them, reaching for their hands. The two brothers shared a look before Arlyn shrugged.

"Mom? How's Briar?" Arlyn finally spoke, knowing that his mother was deeply troubled.

"He's been awake to some degree. He's in pain. He did manage to tell us that whoever it was had struck his bad shoulder. That caused him to go down, as he put it." Bessie was highly worried about her middle son. She didn't know how to help him, other than to pray for him and to leave him in God's hands, no matter how hard that was. As a human and as a mother, she wanted to protect him. She just couldn't do that as she used to do when the boys were small.

"They did? Did we ever check his security feed?" Cayce was worried about that. "I didn't think to."

"Not likely. Joe would have asked for that, didn't he?" Arlyn pulled out his phone. "I have access to it just as you do, Cayce. Let's see what happened." Arlyn searched for the security feed app and signed into it. The three crowded around his phone as he scrolled back through the feed until he reached the spot where they saw Brynne racing for the back door and the man running after her. Then, hours later, they saw Briar being assaulted just inside the front door. They all drew in deep breaths before Arlyn saved the feed and sent it on to Joe.

Joe sighed as he reached for his phone. It had been constantly ringing or chiming. He frowned at the text from Arlyn before he looked at the video feed. Joe nodded as he watched it. It would help. He then forwarded it on to the lab, simply asking them to search for what evidence that they could find.

Ardan found his family and then directed them to the chapel. They needed to spend time in communion with their Heavenly Father and this was one way to do so.

Arlyn walked away at last, heading for his brother. He knew that his mother was heading for Brynne. He was saddened that Brynne didn't have her own family at a time like this but knew that they were likely responsible to some degree for what had happened. That angered him for a moment.

Standing beside his brother, Arlyn struggled to release his anger. Briar should not be lying here as he was, unconscious once more, assaulted again, and with his bride unconscious in another room. That didn't seem fair somehow.

Briar moved restlessly, the pain drawing him up from the darkness. His eyes opened and he looked around, a frown on his face. He didn't remember what happened and had no idea why he was in a hospital bed. Briar shifted to sit on the side of the bed, waiting to gather enough strength to slide down from it and search for his clothes.

Dressed and walking from the room, Briar searched for someone, not sure who it was that he was searching for. He paused at a doorway, eyeing the bed inside and then approaching it. He sighed to himself. This was the lady whom he was searching for. Briar just couldn't remember her name but the wedding band on her finger matched his. He simply crawled up beside her and cradled her to him with his good arm. His head went against her and he slept, a real sleep this time.

Chapter 25

Cayce and Arlyn had come looking for their brother. It was the next morning and they had been through his home, searching for just what they were not sure of. Everything seemed to be normal there. They exchanged glances and then shrugged before heading for Arlyn's truck and then the hospital.

Not finding Briar in his room, the two brothers began to hunt for him, a nurse pointing them towards Brynne's room. They stopped just inside the doorway, not surprised to find him there.

Briar roused as he heard Cayce's voice, not sure why he would be in his home. He sat up, a hand going to his shoulder as pain wafted through him. The pain had eased, thanks to the pain medications, but it was enough to stop him for a moment. Briar stared at his brothers, not certain why they were there.

"Briar? And how are you this morning?" Arlyn grinned at his brother as he stopped just short of him.

"How am I supposed to feel? And how did I get here? I don't remember anything." Briar scowled at his brothers as they laughed quietly at him. "It's not funny, you know." He looked down at Brynne. "And what is wrong with her?"

"You were attacked in your home, Briar. Whoever the men were? They aimed for your bad shoulder and that took you down. You didn't have a chance." Cayce's voice was tight with his anger and worry. "And as for Brynne? She was chased through your back yard, just managing to get inside. She has not roused at all. It's been hours for her."

Briar nodded, a sad look on his face. He thought that he had found her and then sat with her for hours, but he could not be sure on that at all. He looked up at the ceiling, begging God for an end to this. He just didn't think that it would come any time soon.

"Is she okay?" Briar could barely get out his words.

"We don't know, Briar." Arlyn was frustrated at the turn of events. "It's like she's just given up and dropped into some dark well."

Briar nodded. They had talked about that just a few days before that. Brynne had been honest with Briar, telling him plainly that she couldn't take much more of what they were going through. How could she when she didn't know who was after her or even why they would be, unless it had been her family? Briar had simply prayed with her, knowing that he could not protect her, not like he wanted to.

"What happened again?" Briar was having trouble understanding what his brothers were telling him. He slipped from the bed, staggering for a moment before his hand found the raised bed side and managed to clear his head.

"You were attacked in your own home, Briar. And Brynne was chased into the house by someone." Arlyn pulled out his phone, bringing up the screenshots that he had taken. "These are the men."

Briar squinted at the pictures, frowning as he did so. He handed Arlyn back his phone, lost in thought for a moment.

"I don't recognize them. I didn't know that had happened to her. From what little I can remember, she just didn't respond to me. We must have sat in the kitchen for ages. I know that I couldn't have lifted her to her feet." Briar was saddened at that before his anger flickered to life. "I want them, guys. I want them and I want them to pay."

"We know that you do, and so do we." Cayce walked away for a moment to cover his emotions and then to get them under control. He watched as Joe walked towards him before Joe pointed towards the waiting room. Cayce headed that way after he had stared over his shoulder towards the hospital room. "Joe?"

"Where's Briar?" Joe's voice held anger, causing Cayce to narrow his eyes towards him.

"With Brynne. Briar's on his feet. Brynne isn't." Cayce refused to back down from Joe, locked in a stare-down with him.

"That's where I want him. I want them together." Joe abruptly walked away from Cayce and headed for where Briar and Brynne were. He had received word from the street that they were to disappear that day, and Joe was determined to protect them and prevent that at any cost.

Briar turned as Joe entered the room, not sure why the investigator would be there. He then turned back to stare down at Brynne. That lady was not rousing and he wanted her to.

"Briar? We need to find some place to put you two. There is word coming from the streets that you two are to disappear today." Joe's anger had him biting out his words.

"There is? I doubt that there is much that we can do about it, is there?" Briar turned back to Brynne, not hearing Joe continuing to speak with him.

Joe drew in a frustrated breath. He needed Briar's attention and just didn't have it. He shared a look with the other brothers, who simply shrugged. They could not force Briar to do anything. If Joe wanted to try, it was up to him.

"Joe? What else can you tell us?" Arlyn spoke at last, his eyes on his brother.

"Not a lot. It's still very much an active and fluid investigation. That security video is still being looked at." Joe watched Briar once more before he walked away. He couldn't do anything more for now. Joe wanted to put Briar and Brynne somewhere to keep them safe but that wasn't happening at that point.

Briar finally looked around, surprised that Joe had left. He looked at his brothers, who shrugged and then looked at one another.

Brynne had begun to rouse by that time, hearing Briar's voice speaking. She frowned as she listened to him. He wasn't talking to her, she decided. Brynne's eyes opened slightly as she searched the room for that man who had chased her. She couldn't see him. A slight movement from her had Briar turning back to her, a hand resting on her cheek.

Briar couldn't say anything as Brynne reached to grasp his hand. He was just so glad to see her awakening. His two brothers stepped from the room, deep in conversation. Cayce walked away, heading to find his truck, knowing that Briar would want to head for home.

Chapter 26

A week later, Brynne paced through her home. She was too afraid to go outside, afraid that a man would appear to chase her once more and make her disappear. Brynne knew that she couldn't handle being torn from Briar and his family. She heard Briar's footsteps as he moved around the kitchen and smiled. She almost ran that way, needing to be with him.

Briar turned as he felt a hand on his back and wrapped Brynne into his arms. He had been able to leave the sling aside at last, the blows that he had taken when assaulted not doing any further damage despite the pain that he had encountered.

"Okay, love?" Briar stared down as his bride, not sure why she had ran towards him as she had.

"No, I don't know that I am. I'm so afraid, Briar. Does that make sense?" Brynne leaned back to look up at him, reluctant to move away from him.

"Yes, it does. I'm afraid too, love. Despite how much we've prayed for this to be over, it's not. And we don't have any further information as to who or why." Briar was frustrated at that. His friends were working on it and reaching out to others in their search for whoever it was. They just hadn't found the people responsible. Simon had had a thought that he had sent in a text message to Briar just that morning. "Simon had a question." Briar was unsure how to word his next sentence.

"And that would be?" Brynne frowned at him. "What did Simon ask?"

"He wondered if we were forced to marry to keep you safe, not to harm you. He's been looking into your family and those around them and says he doesn't like what he's seeing." Briar shifted on his feet, reaching to turn off the stove burner before the scrambled eggs burned.

"To keep me safe?" Brynne shoved away from Briar to pace through the house once more. She had begun to put her touches in place. The family had cleared out her rental home just a couple of days before with the boxes set in the garage for her to go through. It would take time do that.

Briar moved to watch her before he shook his head and turned back to their breakfast. Setting the plates on the table, he moved to find her, a hand reaching for hers. Instead of heading for the kitchen, Briar bowed his head and begged God to protect his lady.

That afternoon, Briar stood in his work shop, staring around. He was ready to start the next pelt to be done but he really didn't want to start it that late in the day. Brynne was moving around the office area, he knew, tidying up the mail and requests for whatever had come in. He turned as she appeared beside him, a letter in her hand.

"Briar? Who is this? They speak as if they know you." Brynne thrust the letter at him.

He reached for it, his eyes on her. She wasn't upset or afraid, he could tell, just puzzled.

Finally, Briar stared at the letter, turning it to read the signature. He smiled. Someone was reaching out to them and he would certainly respond.

"This man? He runs a foundation that reaches out to encourage people. I met him years ago through one of his employees." Briar hugged Brynne. "We need to talk with Baird and Berneen. They were forced to marry to save Berneen's life. But it wasn't actually an easy life that they had at first. They were threatened and went through an adventure that was really bad."

"Okay, so when?" Brynne walked away from him, heading back to the office. She had almost finished sorting through his paperwork and wanted it done that day. She could hear him moving around in the work room and walked to the doorway to watch him. Brynne was in love with him and he was in love with her. She just didn't feel that she was safe enough for him to be around her.

Briar looked up at that point, dropping the tools that he had been putting away. He walked rapidly to her, drawing her into his hug. He could feel her emotions shaking her body before he turned them to the door. He set the security system and then locked the door after them. Briar walked them to his truck. He tucked Brynne inside before he reached to kiss her. He was deeply in love with his bride, even though it seemed to be too soon.

Parking in their driveway, Briar stared at the truck sitting at the curb before the couple was walking towards him. It was Baird and Berneen. He was glad to see them. Brynne had jumped from the truck to stand beside him, his hand reaching for hers.

———

"Baird? Berneen? I didn't expect to see you. We just got your letter." Briar greeted the couple and then introduced them to Brynne. "Come on in. We're just home from work."

"We can see that." Baird grinned at him. "Barnabas was that concerned about you that he wanted us to find you as soon as we can. Don't worry about a meal, Brynne. We brought something. I hope that was okay."

"It is, very much so." Brynne walked towards the house with Berneen, the two ladies deep in conversation.

"Berneen really wants to speak with Brynne." Baird had sobered. Berneen's brother, Darby, had wanted to come with them but had commitments that prevented that. "I need to talk with you as well, Briar."

"I know that, Baird. Brynne needs to hear your story and that of Brennen and Jaxcy."

"That's so true. They do need to speak with you two but they've been away on vacation." Baird hesitated before he entered the house, sure that he felt eyes watching them. He turned to look around behind him, not seeing anyone who stood out. Baird's eyes rested on the house that he could see faintly through the trees and frowned. He would find out that address and have someone look into it.

Brynne looked up from her meal at last. She had eaten the fried chicken and fixings that went with them almost automatically. She had listened to the conversation between the three seated with her. Brynne could tell that they were friends and she felt very much an outsider. She didn't see Berneen glancing repeatedly at her before she looked at Baird. Baird nodded, knowing what Berneen wanted him to do.

"Briar? Brynne? May we pray with you? That's what will get you through. The prayers of your family and friends bring you right into God's presence. I wish Buckley, our friend and former pastor, was here. He could explain this so much better than we can. Call him, Briar, or else he'll call you. And that is a promise, not a threat." Baird grinned at Briar before he turned to Brynne. "We explained what all of us have gone through that work for the Barnabas Foundation. We have also told you what the Barnabas Foundation stands for. We want to help you, Brynne and Briar. Tell us how we can do that."

Chapter 27

Brynne sat back at last, her eyes on the paperwork that Berneen was shoving towards her across the wooden table top. She knew that she had to take it but she was absolutely terrified of doing that. She felt Briar's hand on her arm before he reached for the paperwork, starting to read through it before handing her each paper as he finished. Brynne scowled at him but he didn't see it. Baird and Berneen shared a look, holding back their laughter. It was just so similar to how they had reacted to one another.

Briar looked up at one point, staring past the couple sitting across from him. He shook his head. He had no idea how this information had been found but it made sense.

"I don't know how you found all this, Baird." Briar turned to Brynne, finding her frowning at the paper that she was reading. "Brynne? What are your thoughts?"

Brynne drew her attention back from the paper, frowning at Briar before her face cleared. She had no idea what she thought and said as much. The other couple simply grinned at her.

"We all worked on it, Brynne. Dallas led us in that, given that he used to be a police investigator." Baird shared a look with Berneen. "It's hard to go through what you're going through. We can understand to some degree. However, you are not alone in walking this path. We are all there for you to help you both in any way. Better than any human being there, God is. He has walked the path ahead of you and knows exactly what you will face. He will not leave you. That is a promise to cling to. At times, it feels as if He has walked away from you but He hasn't. That's when He is the closest to you, covering you with His hand and protecting you. It's Who He is and what He does."

Briar was nodding as Baird was speaking. It echoed what his brother had said and what his friends from Mistletoe had told him. It was just so hard trusting in this way and not being able to solve it. Briar sighed as he turned to watch Brynne, seeing that she was staring steadfastly at Baird, not even seeming to blink as she listened to him. It was disturbing, Briar knew, to hear what their friends had gone through. The wealth that was Brynne's parents was not sparing her anything. In fact, it looked more and more as if they were involved in their adventure to some degree.

Brynne stared down at the page that she was reading. She didn't see the words at all. She was focused instead on Baird and Berneen's story. It had been brutal, she could tell, but she knew that their faith had been strengthened through it. Brynne had also been somewhat shocked at how they had been forced to marry, but she could see that they were deeply in love with one another.

"I don't understand, Berneen. How did you ever find out who was behind it all?" Brynne finally turned to the other lady.

"The guys investigated it and investigated it well. They had help from our friends on the police. Baird and I were the first couple to go through this.

The others faced adventures as bad as us or even worse. We also had support from the Foundation Board and Doc and Anna who took us all under their wings. Will, the police chief, was also a good support. We have a file here, Brynne, that explains it all as to how we found what we did for you."

Brynne nodded before she was on her feet, heading for the front door. She had heard the quiet tap at it and decided it was her turn to answer it. Brynne paused for a moment, her head turning as she heard the conversation in the kitchen. She frowned as she heard what Berneen was stating, deciding that she really needed to look into it. Turning back to the door, Brynne reached for the lock, her hand freezing before she touched it. She backed away, knowing that danger stood just on the other side.

Briar appeared behind her, not sure why Brynne was just standing there, not moving towards the door.

"Brynne? Love? Aren't you answering the door?" Briar was genuinely puzzled at her stance.

"No, we can't. Someone is out there. Whoever it is means to harm us." Brynne spun, shoving Briar back into the kitchen where she grabbed her phone and called for emergency services to respond. She jumped as she heard the thundering at the door increase in volume. "We can't answer the door, Briar. We won't survive if we do."

Baird was on his feet, creeping slowly towards the door. His phone was out as he took what pictures he could without being seen and then crept back to the kitchen. He looked around, seeking somewhere they would all be safe.

"Where can we hide, Briar?" His voice cut through the fog that Briar seemed to be in.

Briar shook his head, coming back to the present. He had been very afraid and almost terrified at Baird's words. He looked up at the ceiling, seeking an answer and not finding one right away. Briar then turned to Baird, not sure what to say.

"I don't know, Baird. I really don't know." Briar spun in a circle, seeking another answer that he could not find.

Baird walked rapidly through the house, seeking somewhere the ladies at least could hide while he and Briar kept them safe. He paused in the office, a frown at the built-in book cases. It would be too easy, he decided, before he was feeling at the book cases. A sudden click startled him before the one book case started to move towards him. Baird opened it fully, glancing into it, and then calling for the others.

Briar spun before he was shoving the two ladies towards the office. The three stopped, dumbstruck, at the opening in the wall before they were running into it. Baird followed, pulling the book case shut behind him. A low light had clicked on as the door closed, bathing the four in light while shadows were around them.

Brynne moved into Briar's arms, afraid of what had happened. She opened her mouth to speak before his finger was laid across it to stop her words. Baird stood near the entrance to the room, Berneen tight to him, as he heard the thudding footsteps and angry words that were sounding through the house. He was positive that he had heard breaking glass as the book case swung shut behind them.

Briar wasn't sure just what was happening in their home. All he could do was pray and beg for protection. His eyes were on the opening, certain that it would open and they would all disappear.

Chapter 28

Joe stood on the sidewalk near his car and watched as three men were led from the house, their wrists handcuffed behind them. He could feel their anger at being arrested inside the house. His attention turned to the officer walking towards him.

"Joe? There's no sign of Briar or Brynne but there are four mugs on the kitchen table. I have no idea where they are." The officer was puzzled. They had arrived on site just in time to find the men still searching the house. They had arrested the men and had stuffed them into the back of the patrol vehicles, ready to take them to the department and sort out what charges that they should face.

"Four mugs? Then, someone was here. And there's no sign of what happened to them?" Joe studied the house, a frown on his face. Where were his friends? And who had been with them?

"No sign at all. I mean, their shoes are there as are shoes that seem to belong to another couple. There is a purse hanging on a chair in the kitchen. And their phones are there. It's just so bizarre." The officer paced back into the house with Joe, watching the crime scene techs as they arrived. "I just wish that I knew where they were."

Joe nodded, doing his own walk through the house. He paused in the office, sensing that someone was there but not seeing anyone. He frowned again before he called for Briar and Brynne. Joe waited and then called for them again, simply stating that it was him.

A sound behind him had him spinning to face that way, his weapon in his hand and raised. He shoved it back into his holster as the book case moved and Briar appeared, followed by Brynne, and then a couple who he didn't recognize.

"Joe? Is it safe?" Brynne peered around Briar, an unsettled look on her face. "We heard them in here. Who are they and where are they?"

"It is as safe as it can be, Brynne. As for the men, they are under arrest and on their way to jail. The responding officers met them coming out of the house as they were entering. Now, what can you tell me? And introduce me to your friends."

Briar nodded, knowing that there was more to it than Joe could tell them at the present time. He looked down at Brynne before looking behind him at Baird and Berneen.

"Not a lot, Joe. This is Baird and Berneen, friends of mine. Baird had heard a sound at the door and headed that way. He came back and then searched for a place for us to hide." Briar turned back to stare at the room where they had taken refuge. "I didn't know that there was a room there. God led Baird to find it. That's our story, Joe."

"And you're sticking to it, I can tell." Joe grinned for a moment before he sobered. "Sounds as if you didn't see much."

———

"Not a lot. I only caught a quick look at the men before I looked for somewhere to hide. I didn't know if there was a hidden room. God directed my hand to find it. I am thankful that He did." Baird wrapped an arm around his wife. "I hate to think of what would have happened if we hadn't found that hiding spot." Baird frowned at Briar, who shook his head slightly. He sighed. There was something else going on, he decided, but he would have to wait to speak with him.

Brynne moved away from the room, searching through her home. There didn't seem to be anything out of order or missing, but she was still afraid. That fear drove her to the front yard where she turned to study her home. A sigh came from her as she walked towards the garage, an officer approaching her.

"There. There's something about the garage that's off." Brynne reached to punch in the code for the door, the officer's hand up to stop her from opening the door. "I need to go in there."

"Not until we search it. Head back into the house." The officer's hand came out to gently grasp her arm, turning her back to the house and then shoving her inside before he motioned to an officer to stand in front of the door. He had a good idea that she would try to come back out and go into the garage.

Joe appeared almost instantly, a question on his face before he walked towards the garage as well. He stood for a moment, eyes searching the area. He sighed as well, knowing that this had just expanded their search.

Standing back at last, Joe stared at the package that sat in front of Briar's truck. He turned as he heard footsteps and found Briar there. That man should not be there but he was.

"What is that?" Briar pointed at the package.

"I have no idea, Briar. Now, back to the house. We need you to stay inside until we find out what this is." Joe shoved Briar from the garage, nodding at a waiting officer who then directed Briar back to the house.

Only Briar wouldn't move. He dug in his feet and waited for Joe to investigate whatever it was. He shook off the officer's hand and moved to where he could stare into the garage, a puzzled look on his face. Baird had appeared to stand in solidarity with him.

"Briar? What did they find?" Baird spoke in a low tone, his eyes searching around them. He could feel someone watching them and that bothered him. He knew only too well how dangerous those watchers could be.

"A package. I don't know what it is in. And I was sure that the garage was locked." Briar shifted on his feet, looking around as well. His eyes landed on Arlyn and Cayce as they stood at the police line, watching the activity. "Arlyn and Cayce are here." Briar walked that way, shaking his head at the questions on his brothers' faces.

"Briar?" Arlyn spoke for the duo. "What is happening? Brynne answered your phone and just said that you needed us here."

"Someone broke in and tried to kidnap us. Baird found a hidden room in my office that I wasn't aware was there. Then, an officer found a package in front of my truck inside a locked garage. It wasn't there when I pulled in. I walked around the truck just to check it out before I locked the door." Briar was greatly troubled at this. He felt a hand hit his back and reached to scoop Brynne tight to him. She had refused to wait in the house when she saw the other brothers there. Berneen had in turn found Baird.

"They what?" Arlyn clamped his lips shut after his exclamation. "What room?"

"There's a hidden room in the office. I never knew about it. Baird said God led him there." Briar shifted on his feet. "We need to get out of sight and we can't go back into the house." He walked away to find Joe, who nodded at Briar's words before Briar was back beside the group, lifting the police tape to let the other three duck underneath it.

Chapter 29

Ardan turned from his office as he heard voices in his house. Bessie was away with Skylor that day and he had not expected anyone to be there. Walking towards the front door, Ardan stopped as he saw the group that had gathered there.

"Sons? What is going on? Baird and Berneen? You're here? I wasn't aware that you were in town. Welcome." Ardan frowned at Briar. "Briar? What happened at your home?"

"Someone broke in and tried to abduct us. Then, there is a package in front of my truck, placed there in a locked garage." Briar was angry, angry that someone had tried that and that his bride was at risk.

"They what?" Ardan was shocked at first, but when he thought about it, he was not surprised. "Where are they?"

"In custody." Baird moved around the kitchen, comfortable enough to do that. Arlyn reached to help make a meal for them.

"That's good. But the package? What was in it?" Ardan stood beside Briar, a hand on his son's shoulder.

"I have no idea, Dad. They hadn't opened it when we left. We had to vacate the house so that the teams could go through it." Briar sighed. "This is not how today was to go. Where is God?" His question didn't require an answer and none was given.

Ardan's hand tightened for a moment on his son's shoulder before he moved to hug Brynne. She hugged him back before moving away, heading for the office and his computer. Berneen walked with her.

"What are you thinking, Brynne?" Berneen perched herself on the edge of the desk.

"That it's my parents behind it all. I just don't know how to prove it." Brynne blinked back tears. Her family should be supporting her but they weren't. She had had no contact with them for years, struggling to survive at college and then when she first started to work.

"May I?" Berneen pointed to the computer, taking Brynne's seat and then signing into her email. "I know a lady who can help. In fact, she's already likely working on it. If your friends from Mistletoe have been in touch with her, then Emma will have material to send you."

"She would? How?" Brynne was puzzled at that. "She doesn't know me or anything about me."

"No, she doesn't, but because you have friends that know her, she will have done this. And there is no charge in this." Berneen smiled up at Brynne who was staring at her in shock. "Emma and Abe went through some pretty brutal stuff as did his security team. We have many friends who would gladly speak with you and tell you their story."

"You do? Maybe I need to do that." Brynne slumped against the desk. "Okay, email her."

Berneen turned back to her email, not surprised to see that Emma had responded to her previous email.

"She's found information for you, Brynne. Let me print it off for you." Berneen was on her feet, heading for the printer. She had printed enough copies for all of them, including Joe, even though she was well aware that Emma would have reached out to him. "Let's eat, Brynne, and then we'll spend time in prayer." She studied the other lady. "God is here, Brynne. He has you in the hollow of His hand. A friend has a saying that God has a plan and purpose for our lives that we don't see. And he is so right about that."

"I guess. Sometimes, it's hard to realize that and then trust in Someone who you can't see."

"It is. I had so many doubts and times of disbelief through our adventure." She pointed towards the doorway. "Come on before the guys eat all the food."

Briar was standing in the hallway, not wanting to interrupt the ladies. Brynne walked into his hug, Berneen slipping by them to find Baird.

"Okay, love?" Briar looked down at her.

"I think so. Berneen has material for us to go over." Brynne looked up at him, seeing the love he had for her on his face and in his eyes. "Briar?"

"We'll talk, love. We'll talk." He kissed her forehead before he turned her towards the kitchen. "We'll eat first. Then, we'll need to spend a long time in prayer. Things are beginning to heat up, as they say, and we need that support."

An hour later, they raised their heads from their time of prayer. Joe had shown up, needing to talk with Briar and Brynne but had taken the plate of food handed to him and then bowed his head to join in the time of prayer.

Berneen was on her feet, heading for the office and then returning with the piles of papers that she distributed to everyone. There was silence in the room as they all read the reports, pens out to mark material that struck them the strongest.

Joe raised his head, a thoughtful look on his face. He had no idea where Emma had found the information that she had. He looked around the group, seeing varying expressions on each face. He watched Brynne the closest, seeing the shuttered look on her face. Joe needed her to speak, he just wasn't sure if she would.

Brynne rose, dropping her papers to the tabletop and walked away. She found a seat on the couch, curling up in a corner of it, an afghan wrapped around her. Brynne was deeply troubled at what she had been reading. She had no idea that her parents were that bad but hiding it so well. Brynne's eyes closed as she struggled with her emotions, not hearing the footsteps that approached her. She jumped as she felt an arm around her before she turned to lean against Briar. He had come to find her, deeply troubled as well at what he had read. He just didn't know how it would affect his bride.

———

Joe had watched the couple walk away. He needed to speak with them about what was in the package. Its contents were deeply troubling, to say the least. Someone had been through their home and gathered items that would mean something to them and placed them in the box as a threat.

Chapter 30

Brynne shifted in Briar's hold, her eyes on Joe as he sat across from them, his notepad and pen out. She knew that he wanted to talk with her. She just wasn't sure if she wanted to speak with him. Her eyes rose to the ceiling, praying for peace, almost begging God for that.

"Brynne? Briar? We need to talk." Joe broke the silence in the room. "I need to go over what was in the package. And we need to do it now." His voice was stern although it did hold a tone of compassion for her. He had seen circumstances like this far too many times.

"I guess that we do." Brynne sighed. She didn't want this. She wanted her life to go back to what it was weeks ago. She just knew that it wouldn't, however. Life had to be lived, no matter how much a person didn't want it to as it was.

"We do, Brynne. Briar? I have a list of items that was in the package. They are all from your home."

"Our home? How? I don't remember seeing anything missing but then if it was done that day, we might not have." Briar closed his eyes, trying to remember what, if anything, that he didn't see. "Brynne?"

"I don't know, Briar. I'm not that familiar with your home so I might not know what was missing. Anything that we packed up from my home is still in boxes in the basement. I haven't sorted through anything yet." Brynne studied her rings. She didn't want to know what was there but she was enough of a realist to know that she would be told.

"So, what was in the package, Joe?" Briar kept his eyes on Brynne, knowing how upset she was and how she was struggling to come to terms with the fact that she really didn't know her home all that well and what all was contained in it. He would do his best to rectify that as soon as possible.

Joe nodded, knowing that the items taken and placed in that package had meaning to Briar and possibly to Brynne. He had no idea if she had placed anything of her own around the house.

"So, to start with, we opened that package. As I said, the items were taken from your home, Briar. I don't know if any of the items belong to Brynne." He reached for the brown envelope that he had set to one side before he opened it and pulled out photos. He leafed through the photos before he handed them over to Briar.

Briar took the photos cautiously. He didn't want to look at them. His home had been violated in more ways than one. Briar knew that God had allowed this and was walking beside them through this adventure or whatever it was called.

Brynne reached to take the photos from Briar, her eyes searching Joe's face and seeing the tightness in it. He was highly disturbed, she could tell. Her eyes dropped to the photos and she looked at each one. She could hear soft sounds from Briar before he took the photos back.

"These are things that tie in with my work, Joe. Sentimental objects from my travels. That doesn't make sense. No one followed me as I traveled. And I haven't traveled in months, not since last year." Briar was genuinely puzzled by that.

"They've been tracking you, Briar, for a number of years. How that ties in with Brynne? We don't have enough information to know that. Tell me where you were with each object. And then, Brynne, you will tell me if you have ever been there at any time."

Briar shook his head, frustrated at what was happening. He began to write on the photos, indicating just where he had purchased each item. He paused at the last one, one that he had purchased in a local town.

"This last one, Joe? I bought it in Oak City just six weeks ago. Someone knew that." Briar felt himself becoming angry. He wanted whoever that was. He then sighed. Vengeance was God's, he knew. He would have to show mercy towards those people and he wasn't sure that he wanted to do that.

Brynne took the last photo, a frown on her face as she studied it. She looked at the date and then froze.

"I was there that day, Briar. I was there. They must have seen us there, connected us somehow, and then the rest is history as they say." Brynne's hand shook as she realized the ramifications of what she was saying.

"You were? What time?" Briar's eyes slid closed. They had been there at the same time and likely had passed one another at some point. "Joe?"

"You were both there at the same time?" Joe made his notes. He knew that there was not likely any chance that security videos would still be available, but that was something that he would be looking into. He pocketed his pen and notepad. "You two need to be very cautious. We don't know exactly who is after you. Yes, Brynne, we suspect your parents but there are likely others involved as well."

Brynne nodded but remained silent. She was sure that her parents were behind everything that was happening but was willing to accept that there were others behind them. She didn't know enough about their business to know if that was the case.

Briar was on his feet, heading out of the house after Joe.

"Joe? Where do we go from here?" Briar crossed his arms across his chest, watching around the neighbourhood.

"You both need to take care. They are starting to come after you harder, and that means that they don't care if you are harmed or killed. I haven't gotten a good enough handle on who or why. Emma has promised to forward some information that she is confirming. She will forward it to you two as well. I would not be surprised to see her appear at some point." Joe drew in a deep breath. "One of the security teams in the area will likely be in touch with you. Emma will see to that."

"I get that, Joe. It's just the unknown. I know that God is leading in this. It's hard to trust in times like this. It's hard to have faith in Someone unseen."

Briar drew in a deep breath. "I need to talk to someone other that Arlyn and Baird."

"You do. Listen. I know of three security teams that live in different towns in the area. Emma's husband, Abe, has one. I can put you in touch with the leaders of the other two, Don and Richard. They and their team members all had adventures similar to what you are going through. Your friends in Mistletoe also went through stuff. Talk to them. Have the ladies talk to Brynne about what they faced."

Briar nodded. Brynne and he had already spoken about that. Baird and Berneen had asked that of them. Brynne had agreed to that.

Chapter 31

Three days later, Briar stood in the centre of his work room, looking around. He didn't think that anyone had been in there, but he could not be certain. They still had no idea how the items had been removed from his home. Evidence was just not there to show it. The only solution to that was that someone had entered their home at some point when they were out in the yard and had not been seen. That disturbed Briar and Brynne greatly. Briar walked the work room, studying his supplies and then the white board that held the list of animals to complete. It was long, he decided, and he no longer felt safe working in his building.

Brynne had seated herself at the desk in the reception area and was working through the accumulated mail. She stared at some of the envelopes, a sense of dread and fear running through her. She would need to open them but not until Briar would be available. At the moment, Brynne didn't want to disturb him.

Two hours later, Brynne was on her feet, heading for the outside. She needed to be outside, she decided, her mug of coffee in her hand. She found the picnic table near the back door and sat, watching the area around her. Brynne sighed to herself. This was not how she had envisioned her life and certainly not married life. She was so engrossed in her thoughts that she didn't feel the hands that landed on her shoulders. She gave a small scream and tried to escape to no avail.

Brynne was dragged to her feet and shoved towards the back door of the building. The door was wrenched open violently, bringing Briar's head around before he dropped the tool that he was holding. On his feet, Briar strode towards Brynne, stopping abruptly and raising his hands. His eyes were locked with those of Brynne. Briar could tell that she was terrified and also that there was nothing at the present time that he could do to relieve her fear or free her.

"What do you want?" Briar's voice was a low growl.

The man didn't speak and also didn't release his hold on Brynne's shoulder. She grimaced from the pain of his grip, refusing to move forward at his nudge until he shoved her forward. Brynne stumbled for a moment, hearing Briar's voice raised in anger. She jerked from the man's hold and ran for Briar, swept into his arms and his tight hold. Brynne spun as best as she could to face the man.

Briar's head turned slightly as he heard noise behind him. He knew that there were other men there behind him even though they had not spoken. He was afraid for his lady and could only beg God for protection for her and then for himself. They stood like this for what felt hours but in reality was just minutes.

Shoved from the building and into a truck, Briar's hand reached for Brynne's, grasping hers tightly in his. She shifted as close to him as her seatbelt would allow. His eyes watched carefully where they were heading, not liking that they were heading for the industrial side of town. His hand tightened on Brynne's hand

"Where are we going?" Brynne finally spoke, anger sparking in her voice.

"Never mind." The man sitting beside her spoke at last. "You're now in our control, and you will do what we say." He sneered at her.

"No, we're not." Brynne's head hit Briar's shoulder at the blow that was launched at her. She could hear the shout of anger from Briar and his shout to leave her alone.

The truck pulled into a bay in a building and Brynne was pulled roughly from the truck. Briar was pulled from the other side and despite his struggles to free his arm and reach Brynne, he just wasn't allowed to. The couple were jerked roughly into a room and the door was slammed after them, the first man standing in front of it. Shoved into chairs situated across the room from one another, the couple stared at one another and then around the room. Neither had any idea of who had done this or why.

Minutes ticked by on the clock on the wall. Briar was beginning to grow desperate to escape, not seeing any opportunity to do just that.

At last, Briar was pulled to his feet and once more shoved forward and through the room door and to another room. He stood, staring at the fox pelt and the tools that lay there. He shook his head. There was no way that he was working on that. Briar had a good suspicion that he would be forced to work on that pelt and that it would be used for smuggling. He was not prepared to take part in that.

Turning his head, Briar's heart sank. Brynne had forcibly been brought into the room and shoved roughly down into a chair. A weapon was held on it in a threatening manner. Brynne didn't move, too frightened to do so. Her eyes pleaded with Briar to do something, except there was nothing that he could do.

After what seemed to be multiple hours, a man entered the room, his evil and cruel eyes landing on Brynne. She didn't know him but he was one of the men who stood behind what was happening. He then turned his attention to Briar, finding that man staring at him, his eyes locking with the man's.

The man, Wright by name, walked towards Briar, stopping at the table. His hand reached for one of the tools, lifting it before he set it back down. He walked around the table before he stood opposite Briar. His angry look didn't change the look on Briar's face, who stood with an impassive look on his face.

"You will work for us, Koyle. You will do what we order you to. Your lady's life is at stake if you don't." The man's angry look drilled into Briar.

Briar didn't react as much as he wanted to. There was no way that he would work for these people, but he had no idea how to avoid it. He didn't turn to face Brynne, knowing what her response would be. There would be fear and anger on her face or in her eyes. She would not want him to do what they wanted but at the present time, he had no idea how he would manage to escape and take Brynne with him.

"No, I don't think so." Briar refused to move, refused to pick up any of the tools of his trade, and refused to take his eyes from the man despite the whimper from Brynne that he could hear from behind him. He didn't dare move, knowing that if he did, it might just mean the worst thing possible for his bride.

"You will work for us, Koyle. And you will start tomorrow." Wright walked away, heading for the office in the building, leaving Briar staring at the cement block wall across from him.

Brynne kept her eyes on Briar, feeling the man walk away from her and lock the closed door behind him. She was on her feet, running for Briar, and found herself wrapped tightly in his arms. Sobs shook both of their bodies before Briar's whispered prayer calmed them.

Chapter 32

Briar raised his head at last, staring down at Brynne. He had no intention of working for the man but he didn't know if he had any options. He released his bride and walked around the table, studying everything that lay on it. There was a form for the fox, the pelt, glass eyes, paint and brushes, and the tools of his trade. Briar knew then that someone had studied his work shop very closely in order to know what tools that he preferred and what material that he used. He was afraid that they would not be allowed to leave, not unless he agreed to work with them.

Brynne studied Briar as he in turn studied the items on the desk. She had no idea what all was there but she could tell that he was deeply troubled. She turned to walk around the room, opening doors and then shutting them. She found a small bathroom behind one door and then closets behind the others. Brynne paused at the door that they had been forced through and tried the knob. It was locked, just as she suspected.

Beginning to beg God for release, Brynne returned to where Briar was still standing, finding herself wrapped into his arms. She shook with fear, knowing that unless Briar agreed to work with that man, they would more than likely die.

"Briar? What are we to do?" Brynne's voice was barely audible. She was afraid that there was a microphone or camera in the room recording them.

"I don't know. What did you find on your investigative walk?" He gave her a quick smile, seeing her tremulous one in return. "God is here with us, Brynne. Make no doubt about that."

"I know that He is. It doesn't make it any easier. There's a washroom behind one door and a small bedroom behind another. Just a bed with some bedding. They've planned for us to be here for a while." Brynne leaned against him, staring at the rudimentary kitchen cabinet and fridge and hot plate. "They've planned for this."

"They have. They have everything here that I need to work with. I just don't want to do it." Briar reached for the form, turning it over in his hands. He paused as he studied the belly of the form, a finger tracing the slit in it that was barely visible. Something had already been placed in there, he decided, and that would be contraband given what he was facing. Briar turned to face Brynne, seeing the sober look on her face.

"Briar? What do we do? We can't get out." Brynne tilted her head back to stare up at the windows. Her gaze turned to the table. If they moved the table to a place under the windows, they would be able to escape. Her gaze then turned to search the walls, a hand drawing Briar with her.

"Brynne? What are you thinking?" Briar shoved her into the bedroom and shut the door. He prayed that there were no cameras in that room.

"That we could move the table under the windows, tie the blankets together and escape. Only they are likely monitoring the room."

"I am sure that they are. And the table is likely bolted to the floor." Briar leaned against the door, discouragement on his face.

"We didn't check, did we?" Brynne moved into his space, her arms wrapping around him. "Briar? Is God here? Is He allowing this?"

"He is, my love. He is. I love you, Brynne, and don't want to lose you. This isn't the time or place to talk about this but we have no idea what is coming up for us. I don't want to lose you, but I want you to know that I will do everything I can to protect you." Briar kissed her forehead, feeling her arms tightening around him.

"You love me? I love you, too, Briar. You're right. This is not the time or place but it is what it is." Brynne moved away from him, staring around the room. She looked up with a frown. The windows were not as high in this room and she wondered at that. Brynne pointed to the windows, a finger to her lips.

Briar stared at her and then up at the windows. He smiled. He knew exactly what she was not saying. If Brynne were to stand on his shoulders, she could reach the windows. The blankets could be used as a rope. He nodded and pulled her back into the main room, heading for the table, leaving the impression that he was studying the items on the top of the table but in fact studying the table legs. They were correct. The legs were bolted to the floor.

———

Brynne continued to search the room, finding the small refrigerator and opening it. It was stocked with cold meat, cheese, and fruit as well as bread and bottles of water and juice. A container of coffee cream was also stuck in there. Whoever had taken them had been prepared for them to stay for a long time. And she wasn't prepared for that.

"Briar? The fridge is stocked. How long do they expect us to stay here?" She turned to face Briar.

Briar raised his head to study her. He shrugged. He had no idea how long that they expected him to stay here. The pelt needed work, and that would take a few days. And it was not an easy process, he was well aware, to do the taxidermy work on the pelt. It took time to do it properly. A sloppy form would draw attention to the fox and that would lead the customs people to find what was stuffed inside of the form.

"I don't know, love. I really don't know. It takes days to do this properly. That's what they want, a proper stuffed fox. That won't raise red flags." Briar's head dropped again as he contemplated their circumstances. He begged God to release them. He just didn't expect it to happen.

"I get that. I'm not prepared to stay here for that long. So, what do we do?" Brynne was angry, angrier than she had ever been. "If this is my family doing this, I want revenge."

"Let God have your anger, Brynne. He knows how you feel. He is allowing this, we both agree on that. Now, come here." He reached out a hand, patiently waiting for Brynne to finally take his and then tugged her to stand beside him. His voice was barely a whisper. "I think that I can fake it long enough for us to try and figure out how to escape or for someone to find us. It's too late in the day now to start anything. Tomorrow, we begin the next act in this play called Life."

Brynne stared at him before she nodded. She could not do anything. She had been taken to force Briar to work with whoever it was.

"I just want this over, Briar. I fear that they will go after your family. I don't want that."

Briar reached for a piece of paper that lay on the tabletop and a pen before his hand drew her to a nearby chair. He dropped to the floor beside her.

"Let's think this through, then. We'll list whoever it is that we can think of and then go from there. They took our phones from us and left them where we were taken from. That can't be helped." Briar sighed, a deep from the toes sigh. He was tired of all this and wanted this over. He couldn't go on with the life that he wanted to live with his lady love until it was.

Chapter 33

The next day, Briar stood once more staring at the fox pelt. He had no intentions of working on it. His only concern was the threat directed at Brynne to force him to. Brynne stood tight to him, their arms around one another. Both were afraid for the other even as they acknowledged that God was in control. They just didn't know how to show mercy in the situation that they found themselves in.

Briar's finger touched the fox pelt. It was not in that great of a condition, he knew, and that concerned him. There was no way that he could make it look as good as he could. It was well beyond his abilities.

The sound of the door unlocking caused both of them to stiffen. Neither Briar nor Brynne turned to face the door even as they heard footsteps behind them. There was more than one person there. The sound of the footsteps stopped behind him for a moment before two sets sounded as the men walked around to face them across the table.

Briar finally raised his eyes, keeping his face neutral as he eyed the two. They were not here for his health or Brynne's health. That much was obvious from the looks on their faces.

"Get to work." The order was barked at him from Wright.

Briar just stood there, a small smile on his face. He had no intention of following those orders. Brynne was prepared for her part in their charade.

"Nope. Not happening. If you want something to pass through customs, you need a better pelt. And those are hard to come by. I can't and won't work with anything that's fresh." Briar knew well how to do his work and was adamant on what he would and would not work with.

Wright stared at him in anger before his hand slammed on the table, causing the tools to jump. Brynne jumped slightly as well, shocked at the anger that was lashing towards them.

"You will work on that one and start on it today." Wright stormed from the room, the other men following him.

Brynne turned to face the door before she leaned against Briar. He had kept facing towards the opposite wall, knowing that he could not do what they asked. He just didn't know what to do. All Briar could do was beg God for protection and deliverance and that in time he could find it. He just wanted it right then. Briar wanted to be free but that obviously was not happening.

Brynne turned to pace the room, something that she had done over and over. She could not sit or rest anywhere. Even her sleep had been restless. She hadn't been able to toss and turn, Briar wrapping her tight in his arms as he too slept a restless sleep.

"Briar? What now? They're not going to accept that, you know." Brynne returned to lean against the table.

"I know that they won't. I just need to come up with a plan. And that's not readily coming to my mind." Briar bit at his lip, a new habit for him. "We're praying for protection and safety, Brynne. I am also praying for how to show them mercy."

"That's an interesting prayer." Brynne looked up at him. "And is it working?"

Briar shrugged. He had no idea if his prayer to show mercy was working. He was too afraid to even think about that.

"I don't know, Brynne. God has to work in my heart to be able to do that." He wrapped her into his arms. "For now, let's see how many verses that we can remember and spend time in prayer." His finger flicked at the fox pelt. "I have no intentions of working with this pelt. I just don't know where that decision will take us."

Day after day passed with Wright appeared mid-morning, expecting to see the fox form taking place. Only it wasn't. He was growing increasingly more angry with Briar, the pressure from his employer growing as well. Wright just didn't understand the integrity of Briar and his compassion for his work.

One day, about a week after they had been taken, Wright's eyes turned to Brynne. He had been ordered not to harm her in any way but that order seemed useless and pointless. If she was threatened or harmed, then Briar would fall into line. He would need to think through how he could threaten her without his employee finding out.

Briar watched Wright closely that day, fear rising in his heart. He sensed that Wright had not been allowed to threaten or harm Brynne but that was about to change. He knew human nature only too well.

Brynne paced the room as she had for so many times. She stopped in the bedroom, her head tilting back as she studied the windows. Something was pushing her that day to escape. Brynne walked back to stand beside Briar, touching his arm lightly and pulling him away from the table that he was soberly studying.

"Briar? We need to escape and do that today." Brynne's voice was a harsh whisper. She wasn't sure if the men were still listening in on them but she didn't want to take any chances.

"We do? It will have to be after dark, my love. The men are likely out there." Briar hugged her tighter to him. "It's a big risk, trying that."

"I don't know that we have any choice." Brynne was adamant on that. Her feelings of great fear were growing more and more each day. They had to leave and leave that day. God was impressing her with that. If they didn't, they would not survive.

Briar followed her, the bedroom door closing behind him. He had searched the room and had not seen any cameras. He was well aware of Briar's fears. He shared them. Briar was surprised that neither of them had been assaulted yet but that would come. He was sure of that. Wright was not the type of person to not do that. Violence and evil emanated from him.

"Why haven't they harmed us?" Brynne spoke just above a whisper.

"I think that they have orders not to. But Wright will not let that stop him. He's getting ready to do that." Briar had thought about this in the darkness of the night and had been praying through it. He felt confident that God was working to free them and he was willing to take a chance. Briar just didn't know if they would manage to escape and stay free.

Brynne nodded, having had the same thoughts. How did they manage to escape? She walked to study the metal door frame, fingering it. She turned to Briar before she had the door open and was through it, searching through the tools on the table. Brynne carefully reached for a knife, hoping that it was not seen on the cameras before she was back inside the bedroom, the door closed behind her.

"Here. We can use this to lock the door. There's enough space between the wall and the frame to stick it in there." Brynne pointed at the area.

"That would work. At least, I think it will." Briar turned her back to the other room, sliding the knife back onto the table, his back to where they had discovered the camera. "We'll leave it here for now, until we need it. They might notice on the camera that it's missing."

Brynne nodded, knowing that Briar was correct. She studied the form, reaching to pick it up.

"Do you think that there is anything in here?"

Briar shrugged, not thinking that there really was. He felt it was more of a test to see if they could make it through customs with something smuggled. And if Briar did the work, then he would be linked to

their crime and that would totally ruin him and his
reputation.

Chapter 34

Darkness seemed to take forever to fall. Briar and Brynne grew more anxious as the day progressed, sure that they would be able to escape. The uncertainty of whether the men would come outside of their usual time grew greater in their minds. They paced the larger room, not looking at the camera, and not touching one another. Both were praying that they could succeed in their attempt to escape.

Once they could see the darkness outside, Briar reached for the blankets, ripping them apart and then tying the strips into a rope. Brynne, in the meanwhile, had retrieved the knife and slid it under the metal door frame, effectively locking the door. She then turned to Briar, finding him waiting for her, the blanket rope in his hands. Brynne took one end and tied it around her waist, her eyes on Briar.

"We pray first, Brynne. We have to. God hasn't said no to this idea but we need His help." Briar was almost desperate with his words. He then had Brynne wrapped in his arms, his head bent as he petitioned that their plan would work.

Looking up at the window when Briar finished, Brynne drew in a deep breath. There was a chance that it would work but there was also a chance that it would fail and she would fall to her death. She turned to Briar, finding him reaching to kiss her and mutter that he loved her even as he begged her to be careful and not fall.

Reaching her foot into his hands, Brynne quickly stepped to his shoulders, her hands reaching out to lean into the wall, keeping her balance as her hands walked up the wall even while Briar raised to his full height. Brynne drew in a deep breath as she reached the window and carefully reached to pull it open. She had to struggle with it but it did open for her, a creak coming from it. The couple froze for a moment, listening for any sound coming from the main room.

Brynne released the blanket rope from where she had tied it around her waist. Maneuvering carefully, she tied off the rope and then cautiously moved away from that side of the window, her fingers turning white from the tight hold that she had on the window. She placed her feet on the window sill in a careful manner. Brynne's eyes then turned to Briar, finding him pulling himself up the wall, his feet hitting the wall carefully as he walked up it. He paused as he reached the top, grasping the hinge on the window.

"Okay, love?" His voice was quiet as he asked his question, watching Brynne as she nodded. He looked around, not seeing anyone and then threw the blanket rope towards the ground. He slipped down it quickly, and turned to watch as Brynne stared down at him and then at the rope. She released the knot and pulled the window as closed as she could before she was shifting carefully to climb down.

Briar's hands reached for Brynne's ankles as he guided to his shoulders before he carefully crouched down and let her drop to the ground. He was on his feet, wrapping her in his arms, a breathed prayer of thanks barely audible. Briar then reached for her hand

and began to run for the chain link fence that lined the parking lot. He had gathered up the blanket rope and carried it in one hand. Their shadows briefly showed in the moonlight before they were at the fence.

Briar turned for a moment, his eyes searching for anyone who meant them harm. He then tugged Brynne with him as he searched for a way to escape without going to the front of the building. His groping hand found what he was looking for, a break in the fence. Briar pulled the fence back enough to allow Brynne to slip through before he followed her. The fence was pulled back into place before Briar reached for Brynne's hand again and they ran from the area, disappearing into the darkness.

Briar had no idea what part of town they were in or how far they were from home. He just headed away from the building, intent on finding somewhere safe for them to hide in until he could find someone who could and would help him.

Brynne finally tugged at Briar's hand, pulling him to a stop before she slumped to the park bench that they were passing. She slumped back on it, her hand still tight in Briar's as he slumped beside her. Their breathing was ragged from their rushing and fear.

Briar looked around, a frown on his face. He knew the area. He just didn't realize that he was that far from home, on the other side of town. Briar looked down at Brynne as best as he could in the darkness. They were the shadow of trees and the moon and stars had trouble shining their light through the canopy of leaves from the mature deciduous trees.

"Where are we, Briar? Do you know?" Brynne leaned against her groom, glancing around with fear in her eyes. Her voice was barely audible.

"I know where we are. We're across town from where we live. It will take us a while to walk there." He bit at his lip. He didn't know if he had the stamina to do that and he was also uncertain if Brynne could either.

"We have to walk there, then." Brynne drew in a deep breath. "Are there any stores that are open and where we can find some water and food?" She dug into her pocket. "I have some money stashed away. They made us leave our wallets in the building."

"They did. I have some change as well." Brynne sighed. "Thanks for being such a good sport, love. That climb was hair raising from my point of view." He grinned at her snort.

"From your point of view? How do you think that it was from my point of view? I was so scared as you were climbing, that I hadn't tied off the rope tight enough." Brynne was on her feet and ready to walk away from what she deemed to be safety. "Can we find a taxi somewhere?"

Briar's arm was around her shoulders, giving her a hug.

"We might be able to. If God wills, we'll find a patrol officer. That would be even better."

"It would be." Brynne's steps were slow. Her feet were beginning to hurt, just from the punishment that she had given them as they ran from the building. "When do you think they'll discover that we're gone?"

"About the time that they usually come around." Briar had no interest in the men any more, now that they were free. "We'll find Joe and let him deal with them." He kept watch as they walked towards their home, knowing that it would take them hours to reach there. Briar didn't know if either of them had the stamina to do that.

"I'm praying that we find an officer. We need to send someone to that building. Do you know where it was?" Brynne was not familiar with the building.

"I do." Briar was troubled at the thought. "It belongs to a friend of the family. I don't know that I can face him."

Chapter 35

An hour later, Briar pulled Brynne to a stop near an open convenience store. He stared at it and then around the area. He couldn't find anything that alarmed him. Brynne leaned into his hug, not sure why he had stopped.

"Briar? Are we going in?" Brynne pointed towards the store.

"In a moment." Briar walked towards the store but instead of going in, he found the phone that was outside of the store. Briar stared at it for a moment before he was digging out change and then stuffing it into the pay phone. Quickly dialling a number, Briar spoke quietly before he hung up the phone. He then headed into the store, Brynne in tow. He quickly found the bottles of water and some food for them, paying for it, and then heading back out into the night.

"Briar? Who did you call?" Brynne uncapped the bottle of water and drank.

"The non-urgent police line. They'll send an unmarked car with someone who knows me. Then, they'll take us somewhere that we will be safe. An officer will do some shopping for us for some clean clothes and whatnot. I'm assured that we'll be safe for now." Briar pointed to a picnic table and seated them at it. They ate their meal as they waited, Briar on edge the whole time. He wanted Brynne out of sight and out of the open and that was not happening at the moment.

Fifteen minutes later, a car pulled up to them and a man stepped out. His identification was out as he approached them. He quickly shuffled the couple to the back seat of his car before he took off, heading for a motel on the other side of town. It was not normal protocol, but in this case, it was necessary.

Entering the motel room, Brynne sighed. She just wanted to be in her own home, not here, not Briar's but the home that had been hers for so many years. That was now in the past, she acknowledged, knowing that she would never walk away from Briar nor he from her. They had had a chance to talk about where they wanted to go and both were determined to make the marriage work, both certain that they were falling in love with one another.

Briar thanked the officer before he shut and locked the door. A bag of clothing had been handed to him before the officer walked away to tour around the area and search for anyone who might mean harm to the couple. He returned to find his seat back in his car, a takeaway cup of coffee in the holder on the console. It would be a long night, he knew, but it was what he did and who he was, to be the one on watch for others.

Brynne stretched out on the bed, pulling the covers over her. She had been able to shower and clean up and then dress in clean clothes. She was grateful for that. Brynne would find the officers who had provided the clothing and thank them.

Briar stood for a moment before he tucked the bedding closer around her shoulders. She had already drifted off to sleep. He turned then to clean up before he was back to sit in a chair near the door. He was intent on staying awake and on guard but his body had different ideas. Briar slept, not hearing Brynne as she rose during the night and then covered him with a blanket. She dropped a kiss on his cheek before she was back under the blankets and sound asleep.

Joe walked towards the motel early the next morning, greeting the officer who had been on watch all night.

"Any incidents?" Joe turned in a circle, not feeling himself watched. That was something that he was thankful for.

"All was quiet." The officer pointed over his shoulder. "I think they were asleep fairly quickly. The lights went out shortly after they locked the door after me."

Joe nodded before he walked over to tap on the motel room door. He waited somewhat impatiently for Briar or Brynne to answer but no answer came. He frowned before he shouted at the officer to head for the office for another key. The officer took one look at him and then ran for the office, returning with the manager. The manager's shaking hand held the key out to Joe, who unlocked the door and then pushed the door open. The room was empty.

Standing in shock, the officer stuttered that he had not slept all night and that he only walked around every hour just in the area to search for anything off. Joe nodded, knowing the integrity of the officer and that what he said was correct. He walked through the motel room, finding no evidence that anyone had been there before he stopped at the bathroom door. The window was open and it was large enough that even Briar would have been able to escape through it. He sighed. This was not what he had expected to find. Now, Joe had to search for the couple again and he had no idea where to start the search.

The chiming of his phone drew his attention to it. With a grumbled complaint, Joe pulled it out and then stared at the name on it. His hand reached to pull the officer back to his car and sent him towards Briar's building.

"Where are you?" Joe's voice bit out in anger but with a hint of fear in it. He was sure that the two had been taken captive again.

"Joe? We weren't safe there. Even with the officer outside of the door, we weren't safe. Someone came to the door at one point and tried to get in. Brynne and I fled through the bathroom window, not the first time we've fled through a window in the last twenty-four hours. We're at home. That's where you'll find us." Briar clicked off the call, tossing his phone onto the kitchen counter.

Staring at him for a moment, Brynne shrugged and then walked away. She searched through the house, certain that someone had been in there but she found no evidence of it. She felt it strange that their phones were now in the house but decided that Briar's family must have retrieved them and returned them to their home.

"Brynne? Did we really do that?" Briar stood in the living room, his hands clasped together on the top of his head.

"We did. And I don't want to do it again. Do you hear me?" Brynne's voice was brittle. She was exhausted, sore from the walk, and desperate to flee from whoever it was that was after them. "We have all that mail to go through as well."

"We do. Here, let's take it into the kitchen. We'll be close to the coffee pot there." He simply wrapped her into a hug and kissed her.

Brynne leaned back to frown up at him before she gave a small smile. She walked into the office and retrieved the stack of mail as well as the letter opener and highlighters. She had no idea what all was in the mail. There were letters there with both hers and Briar's names on it but with no return address. That worried Brynne. She sensed that they meant danger to her and Briar. Brynne felt that they had had enough danger and she wanted it all over with.

Chapter 36

Briar set aside the mail, troubled at the letters that had come from those envelopes. He was on his feet and headed for the door as he heard a faint tap. Joe stepped into the house, a troubled and almost angry look on his face.

"Why did you run?" Joe's voice bit out at Briar.

Briar stared at him without answering before he turned and walked back to the kitchen, finding his seat beside Brynne, praying all the while that he could express what had happened in a way that Joe would understand.

Joe's portfolio hit the table before he reached for a mug and filled it with coffee. He sat, his eyes not moving from Briar's who was staring back at him.

"What happened? We found your building open and empty. Your family has been trying to find you for days now." Joe prayed for his friends, knowing that they had been through something terrible. He could see it on their faces and in their eyes.

"What happened? We were kidnapped from my building and then held captive in a building across town. They wanted me to do taxidermy on a fox. I think it was a test for them to see if they could get it through customs. They had similar or identical equipment and tools for me to use as well as a fox pelt. I have no idea where they got the pelt from but it was a horrible tanning job on it." Briar studied his folded hands, not willing to say much more. "The man who threatened us the most? His name is Wright. I overheard a bit of conversation that he had with someone. I believe that person works for Brynne's family business, but I couldn't say for sure. It was more of an impression than fact."

Joe was making his notes, querying them on what had happened during the days that they were missing and also how they were taken from the building. He frowned at them after a moment.

"Wait a moment. You were locked into the building. You state that there was a washroom and a bedroom. How did you ever manage to escape?" Joe looked up when they didn't respond, finding them watching one another. "Briar? Brynne? How did you get out of the building? It's obvious that you couldn't walk out the front door, not from what you said."

"No, we couldn't. The door into the room was locked." Briar sighed, not sure that he even believed that they had been able to escape. He had felt a hand on his back as he had climbed the wall and then descended. He was also sure that he saw a man keeping Brynne in her place as she balanced on the window. "We made a rope out of the blankets. The window in the bedroom was low enough that Brynne could reach it by standing on my shoulders. She climbed up, tied off the rope, and I climbed up. Then we reversed the way we climbed up as we went down. I don't think we were on our own, Joe. I could feel a hand on my back, and I am certain that a man was keeping Brynne steady as she balanced on the window."

———

Brynne was nodding. It was how she had felt. She too had been certain that she had seen a man watching out for Briar. It had to be God, she decided.

"Briar's family? We need to let them know that we're home." Brynne reached for her phone to send off a swift text to Bessie. "They'll be so worried."

"They are. Your mom was the one who discovered that you were gone. She had stopped by that afternoon to talk to you about something and found the building unlocked but you two gone. Once we did what we had to, she took your phones and brought them here and then Cayce drove your truck back." Joe was puzzled by it all. "They really want you to work for them."

"They do. And if anyone were familiar enough with my work, they would have known that I was the one who had done the taxidermy work. We all have our own style." Briar buried his face in his hands. He was well beyond what he could take on his own. "God needs to end this soon, Joe. We can't do more that we have been. And how do we ever show mercy to those who have wronged us?" He didn't expect any answer and none was given.

Bessie tapped at the front door and then opened it, finding Brynne watching her. She simply hugged the younger lady, praying for her as she did so. Her prayer of praise rose as she turned Brynne back towards the kitchen.

"I can't go in there, Bessie. Joe's talking with Briar." Brynne was almost in tears, her emotions running amok.

"Then, where would you like to go?" Bessie waited patiently for Brynne to respond, her gaze raising to the kitchen doorway as Briar appeared and then reached to hug her son.

"Brynne? Joe needs to talk with you." Briar hugged his bride, dropped a kiss on her temple, and then sent her back into the kitchen. After that, he turned to his mother. "Mom? Where are the others?"

"At work, son. What happened to you?" Bessie tilted her head to study her son.

"We were taken from the building and to an industrial building across town. They wanted me to do taxidermy on a fox pelt. I couldn't do it."

"No, you couldn't." Bessie could hear the quiet conversation from the kitchen. "The family will be here shortly, I would suspect, now that you're home. Dad said that he would pick up something for us all to eat. Then, you both can tell us your story." Bessie walked away at that, heading for Briar's office.

Briar watched her walk away before he walked from the house to find a seat on the front porch. His head dropped into his hands. He was just so afraid for his bride, that she would disappear or be killed. Briar was praying desperately for safety for them both, for wisdom for Joe, and that this adventure would soon be over for them.

Hearing footsteps, Briar's head raised and then he was on his feet, wrapped into his father's arm. He felt as if he was a little boy again with his father able to solve his troubles. Ardan hugged his son, his father prayer whispering in his son's ears.

The other three in the family passed the two men as they headed into the house. Skylor headed for the kitchen, bags of food in her hand that she dropped onto the table. Her eyes studied both Brynne and Joe, praying that she had not interrupted their conversation.

Joe was on his feet, knowing that he had to be elsewhere. He was exhausted, he had to acknowledge, with all the cases that he was working on. He stood for a moment beside his car, his face turned to the warmth of the sun. Dropping his head, Joe eyed the house, praying for his friends. He had no idea where or when this would be over. He just wanted it over for his friends.

Chapter 37

The next day, Briar hesitantly approached his building, Brynne's hand tight in his. He almost tripped over her feet, she was that close to him. Both of them felt fear as they were walking into the building, searching for anyone who would kidnap them again. There was no one that they saw even though they felt as if they were being watched.

The sound of a truck approaching had Briar spinning and then shoving Brynne behind him in an effort to protect her. He squinted against the sun before he smiled. Friends had arrived and perhaps what they had to offer would solve this mystery and free them from the danger that they were facing.

Blackie and Simon dropped down from the truck and headed for the pair, pointing towards the building and rushing them inside. Brynne protested, not knowing what the issue was that caused the two men to do that.

"What is going on? Why do we have to run in here?" Brynne's voice had a bitter, hard tone to it.

"Someone is out there, Brynne." Simon was out of the building and searching, his hand reaching for the man who had hidden near the garbage bin. He yanked him from his cover and shoved him towards the building.

Blackie had appeared, his phone out to call for the authorities. Briar stood outside the building door, holding it open, with Brynne watching from inside. He was ready to jump back inside and lock the door behind him if Blackie ordered them inside.

Joe walked towards the man a little later, nodding his head. He knew who the man was and who he worked for. His investigation had him searching for the very man.

"Simon?" Joe's voice had that man turning to him. "Where did you find him?"

"By the dumpster. He was hiding there and had been for a while." Simon watched the man closely. "I think that Briar and Brynne would have disappeared again and they would not have been seen again."

"I suspect that you are right." Joe nodded as officers moved in to remove the man, despite his protests that he was innocent. "I know who he works for. That person is one of the men behind this adventure or misadventure that Briar and Brynne are facing."

"That's what we are thinking." Blackie turned in a circle. "Someone else is out there."

"I know. There have been rumours that they are to disappear again and this time, they won't come back." Joe turned towards the building, heading that way and pointing into it.

Briar stepped back into the building, an angry look on his face. Brynne had retreated to a seat at the reception desk, her hands on the mail that had accrued. She ignored the conversation around her, sorting through the mail. Her hand froze as she picked up an envelope before she was on her feet and heading for Briar, handing him the letter.

Briar took it, studying her carefully as he did so. He glanced down and sighed. It was similar to the ones that they had found in their mail at home. Without opening it, he handed it over to Joe.

Joe took the letter, not sure why Briar was doing that. When his eyes lit on the envelope, he nodded. He had read the letters that had appeared at their home, direct threats on their lives. He expected this would be one as well.

"How do we keep you two safe?" Joe was worried about them. He walked away, heading for his car where he could have privacy. He was reaching out to friends to find out which security team was available and could watch out for the couple during the day.

Abe Finlay reached for his phone. He had arrived in Briar's town, his wife, Emma, and his business partner and friend, Murphy, with him. Checking his messages, he sent off a quick response before he headed to where he would find Joe.

Joe turned once more, something he felt he was doing too much of lately, to face the truck arriving. He frowned as he walked towards it before he was greeting Abe, Emma, and Murphy.

"That was quick." Joe grinned at them for a moment.

"We were in town. Emma has information that she needs to give to Briar and Brynne." Abe studied the area, including the fact that a police vehicle was just leaving. "What happened?"

"Someone was here to kidnap them again." Joe was angry at that. "I need to finish this investigation without any further harm coming to them."

Emma nodded. She handed over a file folder which Joe took from her, a frown now on his face.

"This should help, Joe. You know how I work. My business is finding information that no one else can find. And I have done that. You'll have to prove it, of course, even though I am a consultant on your force." Emma walked past him to the building, simply opening the door and walking inside to greet the couple who were standing, wrapped in each other's arm, fear on their faces as the door opened.

Abe shook his head before he walked around the building, Murphy walking beside him. They stopped at last beside Blackie and Simon.

"Fellows? What do you know and can tell us?" Abe stood in such a way that he was watching half of the property, Murphy watching the other half.

"That man was here to kidnap them again, we suspect." Simon was frustrated. This was not how the day was to go, he thought. They had information that they needed to go over with the couple, and that wasn't happening right now.

"How be we all go in? Emma has information to share with us all, just as I suspect that you two do." Abe walked away to head for the building door, small clouds of dust kicking up under his feet as he strode over the gravel driveway and parking lot.

The remaining three men shared a look before shrugging and following Abe. Murphy hesitated for a moment to turn and search for whoever it was that was out there. He could not see anyone but someone was there, he was certain of that.

Chapter 38

Abe studied the couple, a frown on his face. They were deep in conversation with Joe and Emma, going over the material that she had provided for them all. Murphy stood beside him, watching Simon and Blackie as they wandered the building, checking out the security of it.

"They're not out of danger, not yet." Murphy kept his voice low.

"They are. We need to bring in our security team for the next few days, at least during the day." Abe walked towards Joe and just stood listening to Emma as she explained what she had found. He shook his head. He had no idea how she found the information that she did but she was always correct with who she named as the main culprit.

Joe turned at last, troubled in his thoughts but determined to prove what Emma and Simon and Blackie had provided to him. He nodded at the group before he left, heading back for his office and his investigations.

Brynne felt overwhelmed for a moment and headed into the work room, not seeing Murphy following her. She paced the room, finally stopping in front of Murphy. She had heard his story and those of his team mates. Brynne was not sure that it was all true but she trusted him.

"What do we do now, Murphy? I want this over." Brynne frowned, a thought crossing her mind.

"How do we go on the offensive? I won't be a victim any more."

"You want to go on the offensive? That's good. It's about time." Murphy grinned at her. "We'll make plans. Our team is ready to walk in and stay with you two during the day. Joe has confirmed that off duty officers are willing to step in as well, particularly at night."

"They will? Okay. So we need to make plans. I know my parents. They are behind this in some way. They don't like anyone to walk away from them. I did that many years ago. They plan and plot and then act." Brynne brushed past him as she headed for the reception area, finding the four men still there and deep in conversation. Her hand rested against Briar's back, stopping his words and causing him to look at her. "We're going on the offensive, Briar. We are taking back our lives." She smirked slightly as he stared down at her, his mouth opening and closing.

"We are? And since when?" Briar tried to control his smile but was unable to. That had been the very idea that the men had come up with.

"Since now. Murphy said that your team is moving in during the day, Abe."

"That's correct." Abe grinned at her. "We're here during the day. I don't think that it will take long to bring them out."

"I pray that you are correct." Brynne leaned against Briar, drawing comfort from the strength that she could feel in him. "What are our plans?"

"Our plans?" Simon grinned at her. "Don't you mean your plans?"

Brynne shook her head, trying hard to control her laughter.

"No, our plans. We can't do this on our own. That's been proven. So, we need to come up with some plans. And that means us being out and about. I'm not hiding any more. They can do their worse, but we'll come through with flying colours." Brynne grew thoughtful. "I don't know where my parents are. I haven't seen them in years. I have heard that they are still in town and still in business. We need to talk to this man." She gave a name, drawing all eyes to her. "Yes, him. He's worked for them for years, but I know that he's not happy with their way of doing business."

"We'll find him, Brynne. That's a promise." Simon walked out of the business, his phone out to make a call to Joe. "That's right, Joe. That's who she's named."

Joe muttered for a moment. He had come across that name and had investigated him, setting him aside as not really that important. He would now have to bring that man in and interrogate him.

Simon returned to the building, finding the group arguing amicably about what they should do. He listened carefully to the plans, nodding to himself as he heard them. They would or should work, he declared, causing them to turn to him, frowns on their faces.

The next day broke sunny and hot. Brynne dressed carefully in a sundress and sandals, turning to find Briar dressed in khakis and a T-shirt. They were ready to start on their plans and that meant they would be out and about. It was a Saturday and Briar had set aside his work for the weekend. He wasn't comfortable working in that building any more, and that deeply troubled him.

"Ready, my love?" Briar reached to kiss her, finding Brynne leaning against him.

"I think so. Can we pray once more? We need God's leading in this." Brynne bit at her lip. "Once more, Briar, how do we show mercy to those who have harmed us?"

"It's difficult. As humans, we can't do that. It is only through God that we can. We've studied the verses about mercy and forgiveness. This is hard, especially for you."

"It is, but it is necessary. Let's head for the down town area. I know that my parents used to have breakfast at that fancy diner every Saturday. I'm not sure if they still do."

"Let's head that way and see if it's still the case." Briar tucked her into his truck, eyeing the surrounding area, feeling someone watching them. Driving away, he nodded to himself. There was a car following them that had been parked down the street from their home.

Pausing before entering the diner, Briar stared down at Brynne, feeling the stress and tenseness in her. He prayed audibly for them both but particularly for her, knowing that she may well be facing her parents for the first time in years. That had to be so difficult.

Brynne searched the room, finding her parents tucked into a corner table, just as they had sat there for so many years. She turned to Briar and led him in the opposite direction, to a booth. She slid in with Briar following her. Her gaze went to the menu. It was not a restaurant that she frequented.

"Your parents are here?" Briar's voice was barely audible.

"They are. Over in that corner." Brynne gave a quick glance, finding her father staring at her in anger. "He's mad."

"I would expect that he is. You're out and about as am I." Briar nodded at Murphy as he slid into the booth across from them. "Murphy?"

"Yeah, I'm here." Murphy didn't say anything else. He didn't have to. Both Briar and Brynne knew exactly what he meant.

"My parents are here, Murphy. Is that why your team is here?" Brynne was challenging him, something that he had fully expected her to do.

"It is. We have received word that you two are in graver danger than you were. By escaping, you have both put a target on your back." Murphy hesitated for a moment. "Wright is dead. When the authorities checked the building, they found his body in the room. The camera showed a man entering it with Wright after Wright had searched for you two. He was murdered, Brynne and Briar. Your escape will not go unpunished."

Chapter 39

Brynne walked through the down town area on Monday. She was watching for her parents or anyone whom she knew who worked for them. Ian and Micah from Abe's team were beside her, not watching her but surveilling the area and people around them. They were watching for anyone who wanted to harm Brynne.

Brynne's thoughts were not on the area or people around her, not really. She remembered what Bessie had told her the day before about the day that the couple had disappeared. Cayce had appeared at the building, extremely worried about his brother. Finding no sign of them but with the door still unlocked and Briar's truck in the parking lot, Cayce had reached out to Joe. They had been surprised to find the couple's phones on the work table as well as their wallets. Joe had frowned at that, desperate to know what had happened to the couple.

Days had passed. Cayce or Arlyn had stopped by the couple's house on a daily basis, walking through it and around it to no avail. The couple had not appeared, not until Joe had received that cryptic call from Briar. The family could not explain to them enough how worried they had been or how much time they and their friends and church family had spent in prayer for them. Bessie acknowledged that God was in control and wanted only their best. He would help them find mercy on those who were chasing them and meaning them harm.

Brynne came back to the present as Ian touched her arm in a light manner. She stared up at him, startled for a moment, having forgotten the two men with her. She knew the other six on the team were around somewhere. Brynne just didn't know where they were.

"Ian?" Brynne's voice was low and broken. She had had enough. Her voice was showing her emotions.

"Someone is out here, Brynne. And very close to us." Ian's hand reached to grab her arm, shoving her forward and towards a shop that she was pushed into and through. Micah was on their heels, pointing towards the back of the store. The owner simply stared at them and shrugged.

Micah hit the back door, finding one of their SUVs waiting there, Luke behind the wheel, Micah wrenched open the back door as Ian rushed Brynne towards the vehicle and then inside. He slammed the door behind them and then slapped at the roof, sending Luke on his way. Micah turned to Abe who had appeared as they emerged from the store.

"Where were they?" Abe continued to search the area, knowing that Brynne had likely just escaped being kidnapped again.

"Too close. Ian, I think, spied them and rushed Brynne away." Micah's finger rested on his ear piece. He grinned. "The three men are in custody. The guys moved in."

"That's great. That are three less that we have to worry about." Abe headed around the building, intent on finding his team. "And there they are." He frowned. "We've had run-ins with those three."

"That's what Nathaniel said. He recognized them as they moved in." Micah's steps slowed as he saw Briar. "Briar's here. Shouldn't he be at work?"

"He should be but he decided to take this week to recover. He has work that he needs to do but felt too troubled to work on them. Briar told me that his emotions effect how he works and he doesn't want what he's feeling coming through in his work."

"That's true. We know how that works, not just from ourselves but from anyone who we've worked with." Abe halted beside Briar, studying him for a moment. "Brynne's safe."

Briar drew in a deep breath. He had been worried about that. Abe's words relieved his mind.

"Who are those men?" Briar nodded towards the men.

"Them? They are men who are hired to kidnap, assault, and even murder victims." Nathaniel watched as Briar's face paled. "We know the men, Briar. We've had run-ins with them. I'm surprised that they are out of prison."

"Someone was bought off or scared off." Joseph's voice was grim as he, Matt, and Murphy joined the group. "And I would suspect that her parents are involved in that."

"That's what Emma has been picking up on." Abe bit at his lip, not certain if he should speak. "Emma's also picked up on the fact that her parents have lost a lot of money lately. They blame Brynne although she is not at fault. They have chosen the wrong path in life." He pointed towards their other vehicle. "Head off there, Briar. Let me have your keys and we'll bring your truck back to your home." Abe took them and headed off with Matt.

"Abe? What really is going on?" Matt turned for a moment to watch as Briar walked away with the other four members of their team.

"What's really going on? I don't know if we have a good idea of that. Joe is working with Emma on a thought that he had. We'll know for sure in a day or so. We just have to keep Briar and Brynne free and alive until then."

"It's that bad, isn't it?" Matt drew in a deep breath. "Family can suck, you know." His own grandfather had been behind what he and his wife, Sarah, had faced.

"They can. Emma's all too familiar with that, given what her step-uncle tried to do to her." Abe fastened his seat belt, a frown on his place. "Matt, where would you go if you were trying to kidnap this couple?"

Matt tapped his fingers on the steering wheel as he waited for a red light to turn to green. His eyes were on the pedestrians before he pointed to one.

"That's her father, isn't it? He was here to watch her taken." Matt's anger flared for a moment.

"That he would be. Emma said that he's very arrogant. She's been talking to people who hate him, she states. And what she's finding out is not to his good." Abe rubbed a finger at a temple, a mild headache beginning. "We need to help bring this couple to justice."

"And that will be difficult, I would suspect." Matt drove through the down town area, watchful for anyone else whom Emma had given them photos for. "This is when it gets so dangerous for them."

"It does. They escaped from the building and shouldn't have." Abe shook his head. "I still can't see how them managed to do that without falling or being hurt."

"God. His angels were there. Brynne said that she was sure that there were angels there helping them and keeping them safe."

Abe nodded, knowing that was likely the case. It was who God was, sending aid to protect His children.

Chapter 40

Brynne's anger was palpable. She knew that she had to release it but didn't want to. She had recognized the picture of the men who had tried to nab her that day. Brynne knew that they worked for her father on a contract basis and had for many years. Turning as she heard footsteps, she found herself swept into Briar's arms. Unable to control her emotions any more, she began to sob, feeling his arms tighten around her, and hearing his prayer just for her.

Briar's head raised as his own anger grew. Enough was enough, he decided. This had to end and end that day if possible. Briar was too much of a realist to know that their adventure would end that day. All he could do was try and find whoever it was. He had begun to doubt that it was her parents. There had to be a way to find out who it was.

Brynne walked away from Briar, feeling bereft as she left the comfort of his arms. She couldn't pray, not any more. She had reached the bottom of what she could handle and anything more would send her to a dark place that she didn't want to go to.

Abe and Joe approached the couple a few hours later. Briar turned to face them, an impassive look on his face. Brynne refused to turn from the sink where she was washing their dishes from the meal that they had tried to eat and failed at miserably.

"Briar? Brynne? We need to talk." Joe waited almost impatiently for Brynne to respond. "Brynne? Ignoring me is not going to work. You will listen to me. If you don't, then I am prepared to place you both in protective custody. You won't like that. You'll be removed to somewhere other than this town." Joe was stern with them, knowing that he had to be.

"And if we leave here before you do that? What do you do then?" Brynne spun at his words, challenging him. She had been pushed past what she could handle.

"For now, there is a patrol vehicle outside of your door and an officer on your back deck. You're not leaving here without us knowing that you are." Joe sighed. "I don't want to do that, Brynne. I really don't. We may have no options."

Abe was nodding. Having protected many people over the years before they started training security teams, he was all too familiar with the emotions that were roiling in Brynne and in Briar as well, he decided.

"It's the truth, Briar. You know what we all went through, even though we are trained in security and protection. God is here, in control, and wanting only the best for you." Abe walked away at that point to take a phone call. He stood where he could watch the couple.

Joe reached for his phone, read the text message, and then tucked his phone away. The men were not talking, not that he expected them to.

"Joe? Where do we go from here? How close are we to solving this?" Briar was at a loss to know where to go or what to do.

<hr>

"I don't know, Briar. I really don't know. We'll do our best to keep you safe. I know that you want to be out and about to draw out whoever it is. That's dangerous. For now, please go about your daily work. You have orders that you need to be working on. Keep Brynne with you. I'll make sure that there are officers there. We have volunteers to do that." Joe finally walked away, not satisfied that he had gotten through to the couple.

Brynne paced around the work room at Briar's building the next day. She was afraid, no, terrified, she decided. Abe's team had left, needing to be at their home base. He had offered to call in a friend who had a security team but she had sent him on his way as she refused that. Briar had opened his mouth to agree with Abe and then snapped it shut. His eyes narrowed as he studied his bride.

She turned to watch Briar, seeing his deep concentration as he plotted out his next work. Briar lifted his head for a moment, a thought catching at his mind. He shrugged and turned back to the pelt that he was studying. Someone had asked him to do a squirrel and he had reluctantly agreed. He didn't like squirrels, alive or dead.

Brynne walked over to lay a hand on his shoulder, causing Briar to jump. He had not expected her to do that. An arm reached out to wrap around her, drawing her closer to him. Briar could feel the fear that was shuddering through her.

"Brynne? Love? What is it?" Briar set aside the tool that he held in his other hand.

"I don't know, Briar. I don't know. I think whatever this is will be over in the next day or so. I fear for our lives, Briar. I don't know if we'll survive." Brynne buried her head against his.

"I feel the same. Now, how do we end this? Your parents? You'll have to face them at some point. We could always find out where they are and face them first." Briar was just talking to try and calm his bride.

"I think that we need to do that. Only, we need someone with us. Who do we ask?" Brynne was lost in thought. She didn't know who they could ask.

"I know of a couple of other men who have security teams. I can reach out to them." Briar groaned as he heard the front door open and close and then someone calling for him. He was on his feet, heading for the reception area to stop and stare at the two men who stood there. "Don? Richard? What are you two doing here? Don't tell me. Abe sent you."

"He did." Richard grinned at him before he stepped to one side. "Introduce us to your bride."

"Brynne?" Briar reached for her hand, having felt her hand on his back. "These two gentlemen are Richard and Don. They're the friends that we were just talking about."

Brynne frowned at them, a questioning look in her eyes.

"How did you know to come at this time?" Brynne refused to back away from her question.

"Abe mentioned that he had to pull back to do the training that they had scheduled. He called us to come and help." Don grinned at her as well. "And before you ask? Both our teams had adventures similar to what you and Briar are going through."

"All of you?" Brynne nodded as they agreed. "Okay, so you have lots of information that you can share. Where are your teams?"

"They're at our office planning." Don paused for a moment. "I have five on my team, all men. Richard has two men and two ladies."

"Ladies in security? Oh, that sounds interesting." Brynne grinned herself as Briar's arms came around her. "Briar?"

"You're not going into security, my love. You have talents that are needed elsewhere." Briar continued to grin despite the elbow dug into his side. "Okay, then, fellows. What are we planning?"

"Can you leave what you're doing at the moment? If not, then we'll wait." Richard walked towards the work room. It was not the first time that he had done that.

"I can. I can't get into my work today. How be we head for our home?" Briar dug into his pocket to find his keys.

"That sounds like a plan." The two men watched as Briar set the security system and then locked the building up tight. They followed him as he drove towards his home, knowing that they may well be the ones who stood between the couple and danger. It would not be the first time that they had done that.

Chapter 41

The next day, Don and Richard's teams scattered through a certain area of the town. Briar and Brynne stood beside the two men, watching the pedestrian traffic nearby.

"Are we all set?" Brynne's voice wavered for a moment.

"We are, Brynne. First, we need to pray for you both." Don led them off.

Richard prayed for them, Brynne feeling as if she could almost touch God's throne during that prayer. She wondered at his words of "I love You" instead of the amen that she expected. Briar told her later that was how Richard always closed off his prayers.

"Where are they?" Brynne stood on her tiptoes and tried to spy the couple who had given birth to her and raised her and then let her run without any contact from them.

"They're here, near the jewelry store. Paul and Timothy have them in view." Don named a man from his team and one from Richard's.

"Okay. Then, we walk towards them, correct?" Briar's eyes caught that of Joe, knowing that Joe and plainclothes officers were in sight as well. He saw Will and Bob, undercover officers who had helped Arlyn, nearby as well. There seemed to be enough people around them to keep them safe, but Briar was too much of a realist to think that would be the case.

The possibility was there that something would happen and one of them would be injured or worse, killed.

Briar and Brynne walked forward, hand in hand, towards the store. Brynne watched for her parents, seeing them suddenly in front of her. They had their backs to her as they spoke with someone. Her hand tightened on Briar's, causing him to look between her and her parents.

"Brynne?" Briar kept his voice low but Don and Richard still heard him.

"That man with them? He doesn't work for them. I think they work for him. He used to come around the house and they seemed subservient to him. Totally unlike their normal demeanour."

"Him?" Briar knew the man and knew his reputation. "Don? Richard?"

"We see him, Briar. The others including Joe are moving in around them. He won't escape. This will end for you in the next little bit." Don stopped walking forward, his hand out to stop the couple. "We'll wait here. Joe seems to have everything under control."

An hour later, Joe walked towards where Don and Richard's teams had gathered. Briar and Brynne were in the middle of the group, who were doing their best to keep them safe, at least until they knew that the culprits had been arrested.

Brynne looked up as the men parted to let Joe through. She was on her feet, hope on her face.

"Joe? Is it finally over?" Briar's voice held the hope that she was feeling.

"It is, Brynne." His hand came out to hold her upright before Briar was there with an arm around her. "We have arrested the bigwigs as we say. The underlings are being tracked down. You're safe to go home without anyone to harm you. Don. Richard. Thank you for being available for today."

"You're so welcome, Joe. It's who we are and what we do." Don spoke for the group. They would escort the couple home, check to see that all was fine at the house, and then head for their own homes.

Late that night, Brynne headed for the back deck. There were only solar lamps alight other than the moon and stars. They seemed brighter that night. Briar looked up from where he sat in the swing, a hand reaching out for her. Brynne snuggled close to him, content to be where she was meant to be. She felt Briar shift before a kiss landed on her temple. Briar was content as well.

"God was good, my love." Briar's voice was quiet, not wanting to disturb the late evening atmosphere.

"He was. I was ready to face my parents. Now? I don't have to. Joe will let us know what they're facing."

"Joe called when you were on the phone with Mom. He's planning on meeting with us in about three days, he said, just to update us on the charges and who all was involved." Briar grew quiet. He was content, he decided, ready to go on with his work with the bride he loved deeply by his side.

———

Three days later, Joe set his mug to one side and searched the living room at Ardan's home. He nodded. They were ready to hear what he had to say.

"Okay, everyone. Ardan, can we spend some time in prayer?" Joe's head dropped as his eyes closed. The time of prayer was one of praise and thankfulness. As it finished, Joe's head raised and he looked around at the family. "You're all interested in why this happened. Brynne? I'm sorry. Your mother passed away just a bit ago. We'll get you to see her, if you wish."

Brynne shook her head. Even in death, she had no interest in seeing her mother. Her feelings of mercy towards her parents were a work in progress. Now, she could not extend that to her mother in life but in death, her mother would face the mercy of God.

"Why did they do what they did?" Brynne's voice was steady but low.

"Why did they do it?" Joe watched as Brynne nodded. "The old story of greed. They had wealth that was given to them by their families. They wanted more and they wanted power. They thought that they had it when they started to work with Arthur Wright. He is deep in crime in this town. He is the one who forced you and Briar to marry. Part of it was for control. We don't know who he wanted to control. Your parents refused to let him control them, even using you as a bargaining tool. I'm sorry that they didn't care enough for you to fight for you. Briar, he wanted your talents as a taxidermist to set up a system of sending out contraband. He felt that if he used you and your legitimate company, then he would be safe and not be discovered. That you would not agree to help wasn't even on the horizon for him."

"That's about what he would think." Briar sighed. "It was all about greed, wasn't it? And how do you show mercy to someone like this?" He didn't expect an answer from anyone.

A year later, Brynne walked towards Briar, the grass soft and cool under her bare feet. They had grown in their love for one another and were thankful that God had brought them together.

Briar turned as he sensed Brynne nearby. He reached for his bride and wrapped her tight to him. She hugged him, her head resting against him.

"Did you talk to Joe yet today?" Briar finally broke through the silence.

"I did. It's all over, he said. The last one took a plea deal. I don't understand any of it." Brynne moved away from him, a hand resting on a blossoming tree. "Do you?"

"Not really. I don't know that we will here on earth." Briar rubbed at his cheek. "God was with us through it all, my love."

"He was. Even when it was the darkest, He was there." Brynne stared up at the blue sky, blinking for a moment. Her emotions were raw that day. It was the anniversary of the day that she had escaped her home and run away. "Where is God's mercy in all this?"

"It's here, Brynne. It's right here. It's hard for us to show mercy in our own strength. God gives us the strength to show His mercy to others. It's Who He is and how He works in our lives. He understands our struggles with this."

"I know that He does. It's hard to understand how mercy works." Brynne turned to look back at the house. "Briar? Are you still planning on moving your business?" This was something that they had talked about over the past year.

"No, I think that I'll keep it where it is. It's been hard at times walking in there but God hasn't told me that I need to move." Briar paced for a moment. "Are you still going to work as a wildlife tech?"

Brynne blinked again. She had gone into that line of work as a rebellion against her parents. She no longer wanted to be part of that.

"No, I don't think so. I don't know what I want to do." She sighed as she moved back into his arms. "I don't want to be doing something like that if we do become parents. It's a stressful, tough job at times."

"It's okay. Whatever you decide is just okay with me. Now, let me take you out for a meal. We haven't done that for a few days." Briar waited patently for Brynne to move.

"No, your parents asked all of us, including your aunt, for a meal. I said yes. I love your family."

"And they love you. So, what time?"

Brynne turned his wrist to glance at his watch.

"In about an hour." She looked around the yard. Both of them had been working in the gardens, changing them to what they wanted. "The yard is looking really good now."

"It is." Briar paused, not knowing how to express his thoughts. "I look around here and remember that we were prayed for in the garden all those years ago. God protected both of us and brought us together. Joe couldn't explain who was behind us being forced to marry."

"It would have been the man behind my parents. He's sadistic and that is something that he would have done." Brynne moved away from Briar, heading for the house. She had a salad to make and needed to do it before they left for his parents.

Brynne felt part of a family, something that she had longed for and prayed for over the years. Briar's family had just opened up to envelope her into their group. She turned as she heard Briar moving around the house, a smile on her face. She was loved and loved in return. God had been merciful to her. It was up to her to show His mercy towards others. And that was a plan that she needed to speak with Briar about. Her family's wealth had been left to her and she wanted to use it for God's glory and to show mercy to those who needed it.

Briar watched Brynne closely, seeing the contentment and happiness in her. He felt the same. God had blessed him with just the bride that he needed. He looked up, a thank you and and I love You whispered into the air.